Amazing
Secrets
of
Hinduism

ED Viswanathan is the author of *Am I a Hindu?*, an international bestseller about Hindu culture that takes the form of a very lively discussion between a fourteen-year-old American-born Indian and his middle-aged father, covering every aspect of Hinduism in ninety chapters. *Am I a Hindu?* has been translated into Hindi (Rupa Publications) and Indonesian.

shrigita8@gmail.com

Amazing
Secrets
of
Hinduism

Hindu Culture
&
Incredible India

ED VISWANATHAN

RUPA

Published by
Rupa Publications India Pvt. Ltd 2019
7/16, Ansari Road, Daryaganj
New Delhi 110002

Sales centres:
Allahabad Bengaluru Chennai
Hyderabad Jaipur Kathmandu
Kolkata Mumbai

ISBN: 978-93-5333-530-4

First impression 2019

10 9 8 7 6 5 4 3 2 1

CONTENTS

PREFACE

Namaste.

Looking at this book, you may ask, 'Why do we need another book about Hinduism?' Excellent question. True, there are already many books, so publishing another one does not make any sense.

Apart from that, my book *Am I A Hindu?*, which I wrote and published for my first son in 1988, is on the bestseller list even today. It is amazing that the book is still a darling, after thirty years. Many universities in the US and Canada use this book in their world religion curriculums.

The whole idea behind writing this book is to educate people about India and Hinduism, providing cultural and historical perspectives in simple sentences—one or two paragraphs answering each topic.

I have purposely limited each answer to a page, since most people have no time or patience to read more than a page at a time. The subjects in this book are arranged in such a way that readers can pick and choose what they want to read, and be done in five minutes.

The aim is to light up a spark of inquiry in the reader—to spark curiosity about India, as well as about Hindu culture. I am certain that the reader, upon reading this book, will have hundreds, if not thousands of further questions.

Through this book I am reminding people of the importance of inquiry. Please do not take anything at face value, or believe everything that comes from hearsay. We have to question everything—even what I have written in my book. We should not accept something just because Lord Krishna or Jesus said it. We should not believe something just because it has been handed down through generations.

There are no superlative or fanatical statements in this book. Not even a statement that you have to be Hindu to attain salvation, nor that Hindus alone have all the answers, nor any statement demeaning or putting down other religions. This book deals with just facts, as stated in the scriptures. Whether these facts are reliable and applicable in the twenty-first century is left to each one of us to decide.

Hinduism remains very complex, especially since there has never been any centralization of the hundreds—perhaps thousands—of schools of thought, branches and sects of Hinduism since its origins in the Indus Valley region of India. No scripture has been rewritten or burnt. All other religions have periodically cleansed their scriptures of disputed statements, calling them blasphemy, and also, at times, harmed or killed people who wrote or preached such statements. These things have practically never happened in Hinduism.

In Hinduism, on one hand you may come across the worship of critters like rats and snakes, and on the other you may find the worship of ideas comparable to the Big Bang Theory, Quantum Mechanics, String Theory and Particle Physics.

In fact, I am openly stating that Hinduism is the result of a slowly developed thinking process. The 'Creation Hymn' in the Rig Veda alone tell us that the Indus Valley dwellers had thousands of questions about creation, as well as about themselves. Everything in Hinduism is discussed, debated, argued, contemplated, and meditated on by Rishis, who were the true scientists of the ancient past.

Their frankness and their capability to withstand open criticism resulted in people in India thinking freely and deeply, as well as making unbelievable contributions to Medicine, Geology, Astronomy, Trigonometry, the Decimal System, etc.

We have to allow our children to ask all kinds of questions. Annoying as it can be to face constant questions, parents should still encourage children to ask them. Shutting down a questioning mentality in children is not good for their mental growth. Unfortunately, in many homes, children are instructed to be quiet and accept what they are told.

I challenge everyone, particularly children, to investigate everything that I have written here, as well as everything written in Hindu scriptures and those of other religions. Once again, please do not accept anything that I have written at face value. Please investigate the truth and validity of everything.

Thanks for reading,

Ed Viswanathan

What Is Hinduism?

Hinduism is a Culture

Hinduism is the culture of Indians in India. Many call it
'a way of life.'

It is not an organized religion like Christianity or Islam. It has no founder. It has no Pope. It has no hierarchy.

Just a lot of scriptures.

Hinduism and Judaism are the Mothers of All Religions in the World

All religions of the world originated from riverbank cultures.

Mother Cultures

Hinduism

Judaism

All Eastern Religions Originated from Hinduism

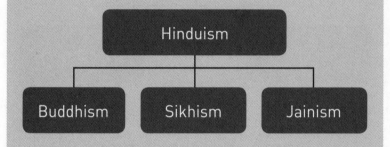

Jainism originated during the time of the Rig Veda.

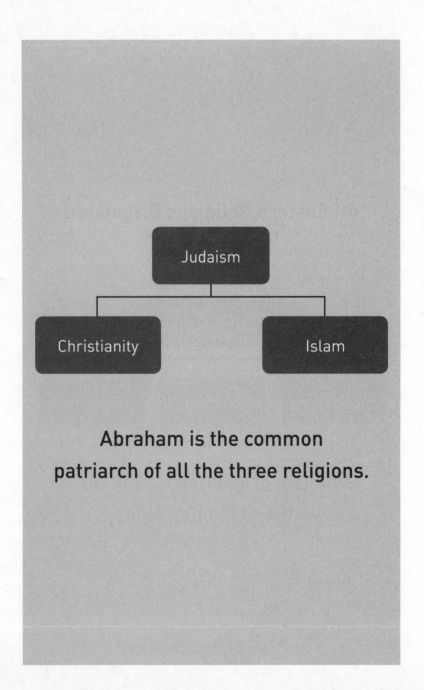

Abraham is the common
patriarch of all the three religions.

World Religion Chart

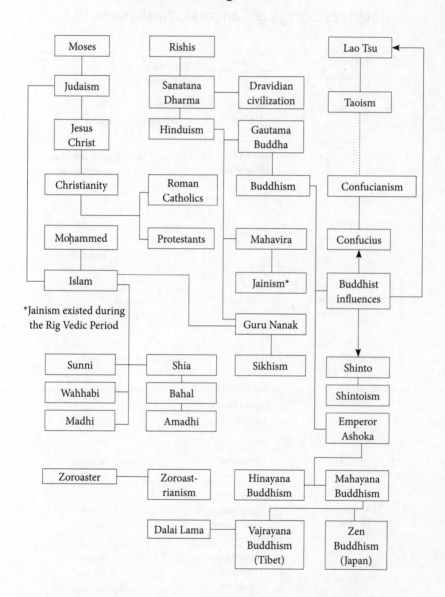

*Jainism existed during the Rig Vedic Period

Hinduism as per History
[Source: Library of Congress, Washington DC]

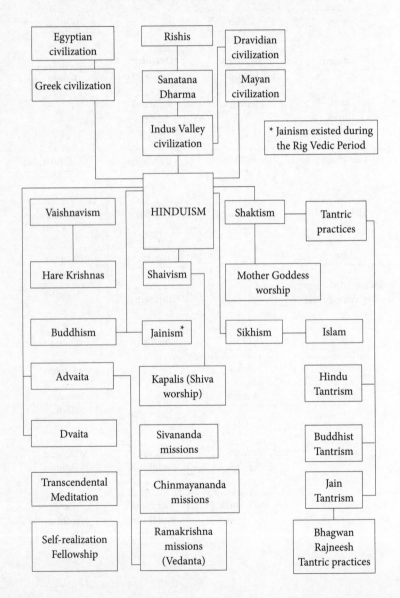

World History Timeline

7000–5500 BCE	BCE	Pre-Harappa Indus Valley Civilization at Mehrgarh site (located near the Bolan Pass near present-day Baluchistan, Pakistan)
3000	BCE	Harappa Civilization
3000	BCE	Egyptian Civilization
2500	BCE	Mohenjo-Daro Civilization
1353	BCE	The Egyptian pharaoh Amenhotep IV adopts a new deity, Aten
1341–1323	BCE	Pharaoh Tutankhamun
1250	BCE	End of the Vedic Era
1250	BCE	Moses led 600,000 Jews out of Egypt
800	**BCE**	**Baudhāyana discovered the Pythagoras Theorem**
700	BCE	Taxila University, the first University in the world
600–680	BCE	Bhaskaracharya, the great mathematician
624–544	BCE	Lord Buddha
568 (approx)	BCE	Jews arrive in Cochin, India
604–531	BCE	Laozi, China
551–479	BCE	Confucius
497–425	BCE	Sri Mahavira of Jainism

470–399	BCE	Socrates
427–347	BCE	Plato
284–322	BCE	Aristotle
400	BCE	Patanjali Yoga Sutra
356–323	BCE	Alexander the Great
322–180	BCE	Maurya Dynasty
304–232	**BCE**	**Ashoka the Great**
370–283	BCE	Kautilya or Chanakya
300	BCE	Acharya Charaka, Father of Medicine
206	BCE	Great Wall of China
105	BCE	Vikramaditya, the emperor
400 BCE–1650 CE		Pandyan Dynasty
300 BCE–1279 CE		Chola Dynasty
44	**BCE**	**Assassination of Julius Caesar (15 March)**
63–64	BCE	Augustus Caesar
64	BCE	Rome burns while Nero fiddles
69–30	BCE	Cleopatra
220–700	CE	Zoroastrianism
272–337	CE	**Roman Emperor Constantine**
275–897	CE	Pallava Dynasty
319–550	CE	Gupta Empire—The Golden age of India
325	CE	**Council of Nicaea, First Christian Council**
476–556	CE	**Aryabhata, who invented zero**

505–587	CE	Varahamihira's tribometry formulas
450–510	CE	Bhartrhari (Grammarian)
543–753	CE	Chalukya Dynasty
606–647	CE	Emperor Harsha
622 AD	CE	Islam founded
788–820	CE	Adi Sankara
1299	CE	Ottoman Empire founded
1017–1137	CE	Ramanuja
1238–1317	CE	Madhava
1336–1646	CE	Vijayanagar Empire
1398–1518	CE	Kabir
1469–1539	CE	Guru Nanak
1486–1533	CE	Chaitanya
1498–1546	CE	Mira Bai
1526–1857	CE	Mughal Empire in India
1858–1947	CE	British Raj
1836–1886	CE	Sri Ramakrishna
1863–1902	CE	Swami Vivekananda
1869–1948	CE	Mahatma Gandhi
Aug 15, 1947	CE	India's Independence Day
1889–1964	CE	Pt. Jawaharlal Nehru, India's first Prime Minister
1875–1950	CE	Sardar Vallabhbhai Patel, India's first deputy Prime Minister

Who Is the Founder of Hinduism?

Nobody in particular.

It is the research output of countless learned men called **Rishis**, who were the scientists of the ancient past.

Hinduism, or **Hindu culture**, has developed over centuries.

When Did Hinduism Start?

Nobody knows.

If you go by the Hindu mythological stories, Hinduism is trillions of years old.

If you go by the research of **Max Muller**, the German philosopher, it is at least 5,000 to 6,000 years old.

Who Is a Hindu?

Since Hinduism is man's everlasting search after truth, anyone who searches after truth is automatically a Hindu.

There is only One God and One Truth.

The very first book of Hindus, named Rig Veda, proclaims, '**Ekam Sat, Viprah Bahudha Vadanti.** (There is only one truth, but men describe it in different ways).'

So a Sikh or a Jain or a Jew or a Christian or a Muslim who is searching after truth is automatically a Hindu.

What Attracts People to Hinduism?

'Utmost freedom of
thoughts and actions.'
That's what attracts
many to Hinduism.

Hinduism never forbids anyone from
questioning its fundamentals.

Even an atheist has the right to condemn
Hinduism in public and still proudly proclaim
that he or she is a Hindu.

What Is the Language in Which the Hindu Scriptures Were Written?

Sanskrit is older than Hebrew and Latin. The first words in the English language came from Sanskrit.

The word **mother** came from the Sanskrit word mata, and **father** came from the Sanskrit word pita, according to the PBS documentary *The Story of English*.

Believe it or not, the word **Geometry** came from the Sanskrit word **Gyaamiti** which means 'measuring the earth.'

The word **Trigonometry** came from the word **Trikonamiti** which means 'measuring triangular forms.'

What Was the Original Name of Hinduism?

Sanatana Dharma.

'**Sanatana**' is a Sanskrit word which means that which is **Anadi** (beginning-less).

It was the **Persians**, who came to India during the sixth century BCE, who came up with the name Hinduism—which means the religion of the people living near the Indus river.

In Persian, the letters **H** and **S** are pronounced almost the same. So they misheard the word **Sindhu** (Sanskrit name for Indus) and started saying Hindu and Hinduism.

There are no such words as Hindu or Hinduism in Hindu scriptures.

'Hindu Law'

Words like **Hindu** and **Hinduism** stuck around after the first British Governer-General, Warren Hastings (1773–1785 CE), enforced 'Hindu law' to rule Hindus in India.

Amazing as it may sound, Hastings also encouraged the study of Sanskrit by European scholars.

Hindu Law is the code of laws used to govern Hindus, Buddhists, Jains, and Sikhs in British India.

Who Were the Rishis?

Rishis were the scientists of the ancient age. They were not preachers, and they allowed even atheists to debate them.

They discussed and debated, like scientists, about every aspect of life.
They even discussed human sexuality.
They explored the universe.
They even allowed atheistic philosophies to prevail in Hinduism.
They never harmed or killed people who put down the Vedas.

Rishis cared only for truth and nothing else.
They did not have any other agenda whatsoever.

Rig Veda 1:89:1 states '*Aano bhadra krtavo yantu vishwatah*' meaning '**Let noble thoughts come to us from every direction.**'

The Rishis did not write, '*Let noble thoughts come to us from India alone.*' Rishis ask us to search for truth all over the universe.

Voltaire said, 'I may not agree with what you say, but I shall defend to my death your right to say it.'

As far as Hinduism is concerned, you have every right to agree as well as disagree with whatsoever is written in Hindu scriptures.

Unlike what happened in other parts of the world, our Rishis even allowed atheists to condemn them as well as to debate them, since the Rishis believed in the immortal words 'Satyamev Jayate', meaning 'Truth alone triumphs, never falsehood.'

What Is Dharma?

The word **Dharma** has multiple meanings in Hinduism. The Sanskrit word Dharma originated from the root word **dhr** which means to 'hold, maintain and keep.'

Dharma also originated from another word **Rta**, meaning the natural order of things that regulates and coordinates the operation of the universe and everything within it. In Rig Veda, the word **Rta** appears more than 390 times.

As times progressed, **Dharma** eventually grew to overshadow **Rta** in the later Vedic and early Hindu literature. **Dharma** includes action, duties, rights, laws, conduct, virtues, and the 'right way of living'.

Status of Women in Hinduism

There are hymns in **Rig Veda** that indicate the high status of women in the Vedic age. **Women were allowed to marry men of their choice through Swayamvara.** Many great women like Sati, Sita, Kunti, Panchali, and Damayanti chose their husbands through **Swayamvara.** Girls were married only after attaining the age of maturity.

During Rig Vedic times, women were treated with respect by men.

In the early Indus Valley civilization, they were treated as equal to or even superior to men. I know it is hard to believe that, since in many places in the world, women are still treated as second class citizens.

Women seers in the Vedas are called **Rishikas.** Some of the great women thinkers and writers from the Vedic age are **Gargi, Maitreyi, Ghosha,** and **Lopamudra. Gargi** composed several hymns that questioned the origin of all existence.

Manu Smriti says: '*Yatra Nari Astu Pujya te, Ramante Tatra Devata*'—meaning 'gods reside in places where a woman is worshiped.'

In India, the Earth is called '**Mother Earth**' and women are considered as goddesses. The chant '**Bharat Mata ki Jai**' means '**Victory to Mother India.**' Bharat Mata (Mother India) is the national personification of India as the mother goddess Durga.

What Are Sruti and Smriti?

According to Hindu scriptures, knowledge (*Jnana*) has always existed in the form of sounds in the universe. Thus, knowledge (*Jnana*) started as **Sruti**—that which is heard.

The Rishis of ancient times, who had perfected themselves, heard eternal truths. They taught those truths to their disciples by telepathy, and later the disciples wrote them in books.

Hindu scriptures are divided into two parts		
Sruti	That which is heard	Vedas and Upanishads
Smriti	That which is remembered	Rest of the scriptures

What Are the Vedas?

The word Veda came from the root word '*vid*' meaning 'to know', and they are considered *apaurusheya* (not of humans); in other words, it is believed that God wrote the Vedas. The Vedas and Upanishads are **Sruti** scriptures.

The Vedas state that self-realization is the one and only goal of human life.

Rig Veda	Knowledge of Hymns	10,600 verses
Sama Veda	Knowledge of Music	1,875 verses
Yajur Veda	Knowledge of Liturgy	3,988 verses
Atharva Veda	Knowledge given by Sage Atharvan	6,000 verses

Each Veda Has Four Sub-divisions

1	Samhitas	Basic texts of hymns to deities, formulas and chants. The word Samhita means 'put together'. Some of the popular Samhitas are Brighu Samhita, Brahma Samhita, etc.
2	Brahmanas	The Brahmanas are in prose and they are concerned with the religious rites and rituals. The Rig Veda has two Brahmanas: Aitereya Brahmana and Shankhayana Brahmana.
3	Aranyakas	Contains mantras and interpretations of rituals—this book is also known as 'the forest book' since it is used by saints who meditate in the forests.
4	Upanishads (108)	Texts revealing ultimate truths from different saints. Upanishads teach men that there is only one God, and that is Brahman—and every one of us is the immortal soul (Atman) that is Brahman.

There is no mention of Atharva Veda in the Bhagavad Gita. Bhagavad Gita only mentions the first three Vedas: Rig, Yajur and Sama.

Rig Veda
1,028 hymns and 10,600 verses

Rig Veda is organized in **ten books** called 'Mandalas' (meaning circles in Sanskrit). Rig Veda is the foremost book of Hindus. **Rig Veda is older than Gilgamesh (2500 BCE) and the Old Testament of the Holy Bible.**

Rig Vedic hymns are dedicated to various deities, such as **Prithvi** (Earth); **Vac** (the word Aum); **Surya** (the sun god); **Indra** (the god of heaven), **Agni** (sacrificial fire), **Soma** (a **ritualistic drink**), **Rudra** (the god of wind and hunting), who later became Lord Shiva, **Brihaspati** (a Vedic era sage who counseled the gods); **Vishnu** (the god of preservation in the Hindu Trinity) and many more.

The Gayatri Mantra, produced by Rishi Viswamitra, is in Rig Veda. The **varna system or caste system** originated in Rig Veda. The 'Creation Hymn' in Rig Veda clearly shows a budding society looking for answers to the paradox of the origin of the universe.

Questions about the Origin of Creation

When people settled down on the **banks of the rivers Indus, Ganges and Brahmaputra,** like everybody else on earth, the first thing they did was start cultivation. Then they looked at the stars and asked questions about the paradox of the origin of creation. Rig Veda hymn 10:129 clearly indicates a desperate search for answers to questions such as **Who are we? Why we are here?** etc.

Like scientists of today, 6,000 years ago, Indus Valley dwellers also asked: **How could the universe have sprung into existence? Did it come out of nothing? How is that possible?**

Who really knows, when and how did creation start?
Who really knows, who can truly say; when and how creation started?
Only He, up there really knows, maybe;
Or perhaps not even He.

(Rig Veda 10:129:1-7)

The Mysterious Soma Ritual

Everything about **Soma** is somewhat mysterious. **Soma** is a ritualistic hallucinatory drink, frequently mentioned in the Rig Veda in the chapter **Soma Mandala**. Rig Veda calls its source the plant of the 'God of Gods'.

Soma juice is prepared by extracting juice from the stalks of certain plant of mushroom origin. A similar plant named *Haoma* is mentioned in the Zoroastrian scripture *Avesta.*

Soma juice is different from the regular alcoholic drink available in ancient India, called *Sura* in Sanskrit.

Lord Krishna said:
'Those who are well versed in three Vedas
(Rig, Sama & Yajur) and **drinkers of the Soma juice**;
seeking heavenly planets, they worship me indirectly.
Purified of their sinful nature, they take birth
on the pious heavenly planet of Indra,
where they enjoy godly delights.'

(Bhagavad Gita 9:20)

Sama Veda
1,875 verses

Sama Veda is a Sanskrit word consisting of two words: **Saman** or 'melody' and **Veda** or 'knowledge'. It is also called the **Veda of chants.** It is the third of the four Vedas. It is a storehouse of melodious chants.

Two very important Upanishads of Hinduism came from Sama Veda—the **Chandogya Upanishad** and **the Kena Upanishad.** Sama Veda starts with a prayer to Agni (fire).

Yajur Veda
3,988 verses

The Yajur Veda takes its name from **yajus**, which means **'yagna'** or 'ritual'.

Unlike Sama Veda, this Veda is full of prose. It describes the way in which religious rituals and sacred ceremonies should be performed. **Yajur Veda deals with prayers and specific instructions for devotional sacrifices** as well as with instructions for sacrificial rituals.

Atharva Veda
730 hymns

Atharva Veda was composed by the descendants of Rishi Atharvan. Atharva Veda is a collection of about 6,000 mantras, divided into twenty books. Atharva Veda is sometimes called the **Veda of magical formulas**.

Even though the Bhagavad Gita failed to mention Atharva Veda, three very important Upanishads—**Mundaka Upanishad, Mandukya Upanishad,** and **Prashna Upanishad**—originated from this Veda.

Atharva Veda stands apart from the other three Vedas since it deals with subjects like diseases and their cures; rites for prolonging life; rites for fulfilling one's desires; building construction; trade and commerce; penances; black magic etc.

Ayurveda—The Science of Life

Ayurveda is called an Upa Veda of **Atharva Veda**. It was originally recorded as an oral tradition more than 5,000 years ago in the Sanskrit language. The three principle texts associated with Ayurveda are **Charaka Samhita, Sushruta Samhita,** and **Bhela Samhita.**

It was propagated by **Dhanvantari**, who appears in the Vedas and Puranas as the physician of the gods (devas) and is considered the god of Ayurveda.

Other than Dhanvantari, other promotors and authors of Ayurveda are **Charaka, Sushruta, Vagbhata, Sharngadhara, Bhavamishra and Madhava.**

Ayurveda describes three fundamental energies that govern our inner and outer environments: **Vata** (Wind), **Pitta** (Fire), and **Kapha** (Earth). According to Ayurveda these primary forces are responsible for the characteristics of our mind and body.

108 Upanishads

Upanishads are the brains of Hinduism.

The word Upanishad can be broken down into upa (near) ni (down) shad (sit) meaning that the teachings of the Upanishads were conveyed from masters to students when students sat right next to masters, and nobody overheard those teachings.

Although there are more than 108 Upanishads, thirteen Upanishads are considered very important.

They are the Chandogya, Kena, Aitareya, Kaushitaki, Katha, Mundaka, Taittriyaka, Brihadaranyaka, Svetasvatara, Isa, Prasna, Mandukya and the Maitri Upanishads.

Darshanas
Six Philosophies of Hinduism

Six Hindu philosophies are collectively called **Darshanas**.

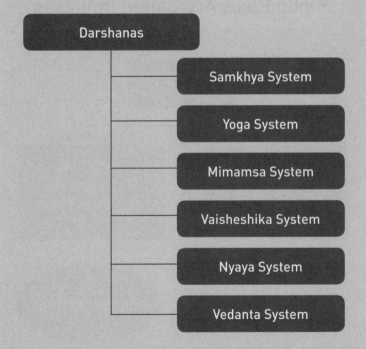

Darshanas
- Samkhya System
- Yoga System
- Mimamsa System
- Vaisheshika System
- Nyaya System
- Vedanta System

It is worth noting that Lord Krishna discusses Samkhya philosophy, which does not mention God at all, at several points in the Bhagavad Gita (starting with 2:39). The only other philosophies he mentions are Yoga and Vedanta.

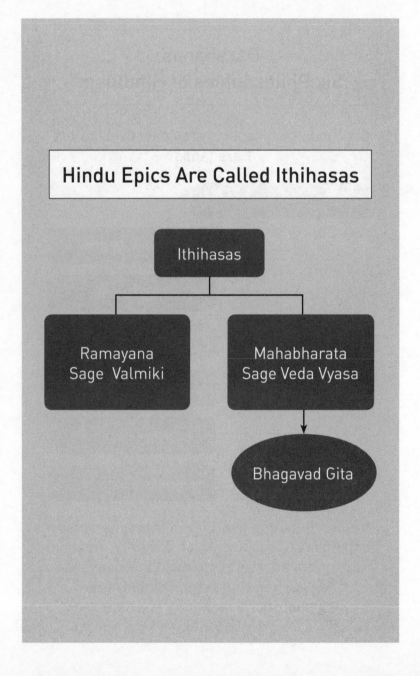

Ramayana

The **Ramayana** is an epic poem about Lord Rama and Sita written by the Hindu sage **Valmiki**. Ramayana consists of **24,000 verses divided into seven Kandas or Chapters.**

Sage Valmiki framed the whole poem as the **narration of a mourning dove** (who just lost her lover to a hunter's wicked arrow) telling him the story of Lord Rama and Sita.

That is the reason you see **Valmiki pleading with the crying dove** to tell him the story of Rama at the beginning of every chapter.

Mahabharata

Mahabharata, written by **Rishi Veda Vyasa** with the help of **Lord Ganesh,** is the story of Pandvas and Kauravas. **Bhagavad Gita** appears in the middle of this scripture. **It is lengthier than Homer's Odyssey.**

It consists of episodes, dialogues, stories, discourses, and sermons.

It contains 110,000 couplets or **220,000 lines** in eighteen **Parvas.**

Puranas

Puranas are religious stories which expound truths. The word Puranas literally means in Sanskrit ancient, old. The term Purana appears in the Atharva Veda.

There are **eighteen major Puranas,** out of which six are addressed to **Lord Vishnu,** six addressed to **Lord Shiva,** and six addressed to **Lord Brahma.** Apart from the eighteen major Puranas there are twenty-two minor Puranas.

Veda Vyasa, the narrator of the epic **Mahabharata,** is the compiler of the Puranas. Among all the Puranas, the **Srimad Bhagavata Purana** is the most important.

Puranas discuss a wide range of topics including music, dance, yoga, culture, cosmology, genealogy, and geography. Puranas are the Vedas for the common folk, since they expound truths through stories and legends. **Just like the parables told by Jesus Christ, these stories are told to common folks to help them grasp the teachings of the Upanishads or the Darshanas.**

The Dharma Shastras

Hindu Dharma Shastras are also known as 'Dharma Sutras'. They are the codes of law that includes both secular and religious subjects such as codes of conduct, civil and criminal law, and punishment.

The most important Smritis are:

Manu Smriti
Yajnavalkya Smiriti
Parasara Smriti
Narada Smriti
Gautama Smriti

Manu Smriti
(Laws of Manu)

Of all the Dharma Shastras, **Manu Smriti** (Laws of Manu), written by Manu, is the most important. **Manu** was the first law giver in Hinduism, just as **Moses** was the first law giver in Judaism.

The **Manu Smriti** contains **2,700 verses divided into twelve chapters.** Manu Smriti deals with all sorts of topics, including **cosmology, sacraments, Upanayana** (initiation), **Varna system** (Caste system), **funeral rites, Ashramas, inheritance, adoption,** as well as the conduct of women and wives.

Laws that were proposed by Manu regarding human conduct and society are not at all applicable in the twenty first century.

Even though Manu has stated: '**...where women are revered the gods rejoice, but where they are not, no sacred rite bears any fruit,**' he has also proposed a very subordinate status to women in other verses, **limiting their liberty.**

Agamas

Agamas means 'scriptures' They are a group of literature dealing with the worship of God in many forms, and they prescribe detailed courses of discipline for the devotee. Agama scriptures describe cosmology, Hindu philosophies, meditation and practices, all four Yogas, mantras, mandalas, temple construction, and deity worship.

Like Upanishads, there are many Agamas. They can be broadly divided into three groups according to the deity that forms the object of worship—Vishnu, Shiva, or Shakti. These three groups of Agamas have given rise to the three main branches of Hinduism, mainly Vaishnavism, Shaivism and Shaktism.

Arthashastra

Arthashastra is a code of ethics for kings that talks about intelligence collection, covert operations, and maintaining the security of the state, written by the prime minister of the Mauryan empire, **Kautilya** or **Chanakya** (370-283 BCE).

Kautilya was a **professor at the Taxila University** (the world's first University) before he became the prime minister of the Mauryan empire.

In some ways, this book will remind you of another popular book, *The Art of War,* by the ancient military strategist Sun Tzu.

Apart from teaching the king an efficient system of espionage, it explores issues relating to society, such as how to deal with famine, epidemics, and acts of nature.

This scripture was considered lost by scholars for a very long time, just like the Dead Sea Scrolls. It was discovered in 1905.

Yoga Vasistha
29,000 verses

Yoga Vasistha is one of the most important works in Hindu philosophy. It is believed by some to have been written during the seventh century CE, although since this book emerged from the epic Ramayana, many believe that Valmiki wrote this book as well.

Yoga Vasistha contains 29,000 verses. All aspects of Darhsanas (Hindu philosophies), from Samkhya to Vedanta, are intricately woven into the Yoga Vasishtha. The principal figures in this book are Lord Rama and Sage Vasistha.

Just like the Bhagavad Gita, this is a dialogue, this time between Vasistha and Lord Rama. Vasistha advises Rama on all aspects of life. Vasistha is an important figure in Hinduism. Manu refers to him as one of the exponents of Hinduism.

Adi Sankaracharya refers to him as the first sage of the Vedanta school. One of the most important parts of the Yoga Vasistha is the doctrine of mind.

Ashtavakra Gita

The **Ashtavakra Gita**, also known as **Ashtavakra Samhita**, is a very ancient spiritual document of great purity and power. It is written as a very lively dialogue between **King Janaka**, the father of **Sita Devi**, with sage **Ashtavakra** (meaning saint with eight curves in his body).

Ashtavakra Gita is based on **Vedanta**. Who actually wrote Ashtavakra Gita? We do not know.

Ashtavakra Gita starts with King Janaka asking the sage Ashtavakra how he can attain knowledge, detachment, and liberation.

This scripture contains twenty chapters and 285 verses. Chapter 18 is the largest with 100 verses, followed by Chapters 2 and 25. Three chapters contain only four verses each.

Rishi Ashtavakra told King Janaka:

'Oh! Mighty king, there is no need to look high for the stars to get answers. They are already within you. Just reach deep within yourself and find out all the answers.'

'Know Thyself' is a phrase repeatedly used by Socrates and also an inscription at the Oracle of Delphi in ancient Greece, which was used to discuss **the importance of getting to know oneself.**

Sri Aurobindo said, 'Listen to your inner voice.'

The Holy Bible (King James version) says:
'...behold, the Kingdom of God is within you.'
(Luke 17:21)

The Hindu Scriptures in a Nutshell

Shruti Literature (That which is heard)

Four Vedas	Each Veda consists of:
Rig Veda: Knowledge of Hymns—10,589 verses	1. **Samhitas:** Basic texts of hymns to deities, formulas and chants
Sama Veda: Knowledge of Music—1,875 verses	2. **Brahmanas:** Performance of rituals
Yajur Veda: Knowledge of Liturgy- 3,988 verses	3. **Aranyakas:** Mantras and interpretation of faith
Atharva Veda: Knowledge given by Sage Atharva—6,000 verses	4. **Upanishads:** Texts revealing ultimate truths from different saints

Upanishads (108)

- Isa
- Kena
- Katha
- Prasna
- Mundaka
- Mandukya
- Aitareya
- Tatttiriya
- Chandoga
- Brihad-Aranyaka
- Kaushitaki
- Shvetashatara
- Maitri

Smriti Literature
(That which is remembered)

Vedanga (6)

Dharma Sutra:
A—Manu Smriti
B—Gautama Smriti
C—Yajnavalkya Smriti
• **Jyothisha**—Astronomy and Astrology
• **Kalpa**—Ritual and Legal
• **Siksha**—Phonetics
• **Chhandas**—Measurements
• **Nirukta**—Etymology
• **Vyakarana**—Grammar

Darshanas—Hindu Philosophy (6)

• Nyaya: by sage Gautama—Nyaya Sutras
• Vaisheshika: by sage Kamada—Vaiseshika Sutra
• Samkhya: by Kapila
• Yoga: by Patanjali—Patanjali Yoga Sutra
• Mimamsa: by sage Jaimini—Mimamsa Sutra
• Vedanta: by sage Veda Vyasa—Brahma Sutra or Vedanta
  Sutra
  – Advaita: by Adi Sankara
  – Upadesasahasri, Vivekachoodamani, etc.
  – Dvaita: by Madhava and Ramanuja

Ithihasas/Epics (2)

- Ramayana: by sage Valmiki—consists of 24,000 couplets
- Mahabharata: by sage Veda Vyasa—220,000 verses, eighteen chapters
- Bhagavad Gita—Part of the Mahabharata, consists of 18 chapters and 700 verses. (Some authors consider this scripture as both Smriti and Sruti).

Puranas (18 are most important)

- Agni
- Bhagavata
- Bhavishya
- Brahma
- Brahmanda
- Brahmavaivarta
- Garuda
- Harivamsha
- Kurma
- Linga
- Markandeya
- Matsya
- Narada
- Padma
- Skanda
- Shiva
- Vamana
- Varaha
- Vayu
- Vishnu

Upavedas

- Ayurveda: consists of more than 100,000 verses, still attached to Atharva Veda; Hindu science of health and longevity
- Dhanurveda: Hindu science of archery and war
- Ghandarva Veda: Hindu science of music
- Arthashastra: Hindu science of royal governance

Tantra

- Mantras
- Yantras
- Mandalas
- Nyasa
- Mudras
- Kundalini
- Yogic Exercises

Agama

- Vaishnava/Vishnu Samhita—worship God as Lord Vishnu
- Shaiva—worship God as Lord Shiva
- Shakti—worship God as Mother Goddess

Upanga: Logical and ritualistic form of thought

Charvaka: Materialistic philosophy which did not recognize the authority of the Vedas—its founder was Charvaka.

What Is the Hindu Holy Bible?

Hindus do not have a Holy Bible like Christians and Muslims do.

Hindus have many scriptures and all of them are equally important. But many consider the **Bhagavad Gita** to be the Holy Bible of Hindus.

Bhagavad Gita appears in the middle of the epic poem **Mahabharata. Bhagavad Gita has 700 verses in eighteen chapters.**

It is in the form of a conversation between **warrior king Arjuna** and **Lord Krishna,** in the middle of the battlefield at the outset of the Kurukshetra War.

As Lord Krishna discusses **over fifty subjects** in the Bhagavad Gita, **it should be read and studied subject-wise.** This is precisely what I have done in my book, *Amazing Secrets of the Bhagavad Gita*, in sixty-three chapters (each covering a distinct subject).

Did the Father of the Atomic Bomb Really Quote the Bhagavad Gita?

In the middle of the research and development of the first atomic bomb, **Robert Oppenheimer, the father of the atom bomb,** studied the Bhagavad Gita and later quoted the following verse from it when the first atomic bomb was detonated on 16 July 1945.

Lord Krishna said:

'I am death, the mighty destroyer of the worlds.
I have come to destroy these people. Even without
you taking part, all the soldiers of opposing army
(Kauravas) will be slain.'

(Bhagavad Gita 11:32)

Who's Who of the Mahabharata

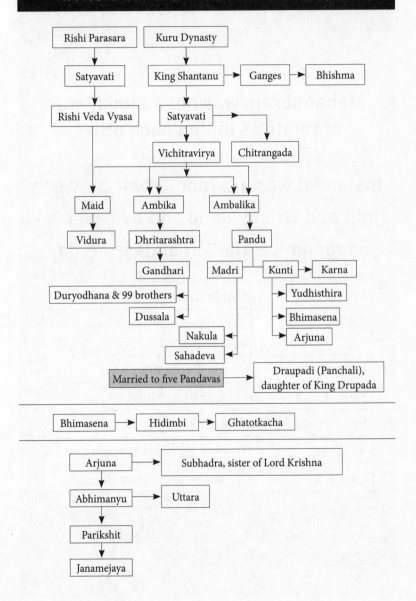

Mahabharata was not a bloody war of relatives killing each other.

Instead it was a symbolic war between right and wrong, good and bad, which is happening within all of us everyday.

Character	Symbolizes
Arjuna	Jeevathman or immortal soul within the body
Lord Krishna	God or Paramathman
Kurushetra	Field of action (life)
Five heroes	Five sense organs
Pandavas	Positive spiritual thoughts
Kauravas	Negative destructive thoughts

Lord Krishna never said **someone will burn in Hell for eternity.**

- In the Bhagavad Gita, Lord Krishna never **judged or ordered**.

- Lord Krishna acted like a psychiatrist in the Bhagavad Gita. First, he allowed Arjuna to present all kinds of arguments as to why Arjuna should not fight this war. **He did not interrupt Arjuna when the latter was talking.** Only when Arjuna said: 'I am totally confused and I cannot even wield my bow and arrow,' did Lord Krishna start talking to Arjuna.

- He only explained to Arjuna **the pros and cons of every issue**, and it was left to Arjuna whether to follow his teachings or not.

- Lord Krishna did not even influence the free will of Arjuna. **Arjuna** had the **right to accept** everything Lord Krishna taught **or reject all of it**.

In fact, at the end of Mahabharata, **Rishi Veda Vyasa** has to teach a very disheartened **Arjuna** the whole of Bhagavad Gita all over again.

Who is Rishi Veda Vyasa?

Vyasa in Sanskrit means to **differentiate or split or describe**. That is the reason why he is called Veda Vyasa, or '**Splitter of the Vedas**'.

He is the author of the epic Mahabharata, the Brahma Sutras, and a proponent of Advaita philosophy. Many consider him to be the author of the eighteen Puranas including the Srimad Bhagavatam.

He was the **son of Rishi Parasara** and the fisher woman **Satyavati**. He was called **Krishna Dvaipāyana** (referring to his black skin colour and his birthplace, the island of Dvipa) initially.

To Hinduism, he is what Abraham is to Judaism, Christianity, and Islam. He is the father of **King Dhartharashtra of the Kauravas** as well as **King Pandu of the Pandavas**.

Cārvāka Atheistic Philosophy

While the rest of the world burned and killed people for disagreeing over what a church or a mosque taught, in Hinduism, we allowed and supported an atheistic philosophy.

Cārvāka atheistic philosophy rejected the existence of God and considered religion as an aberration.

Cārvāka atheistic philosophy preached:

1. All things are made of earth, air, fire and water.

2. That which cannot be perceived does not exist; to exist means to be perceivable.

3. Heaven and Hell are nothing but inventions. The only goal of humans is to enjoy pleasures and avoid pain.

4. Vedas are written by buffoons.

What Is the Hindu Concept of God?

Hindus believe in One God, Brahman, which expresses itself in trillions of forms.

Some Hindus do not believe God has a human form or any other form. The scriptures generally do not ascribe a specific form to God.

However, the Rig Veda does contain the puzzling image of 'Purusha', who has a thousand heads, a thousand eyes and a thousand feet, envelops the world from all sides, and extends in all ten directions.

God is nameless and timeless.

But there is nothing wrong in worshipping a God with name and form (nama-roopa), since man cannot conceive of anything without any name and form.

Adi Sankara wrote in the Vivekachudamani: 'Brahman or God alone is truth, the world is unreal, and ultimately there is no difference between Brahman (God) and the individual self (Atman).'

Hindus worship One God, Brahman, with many names and in many forms

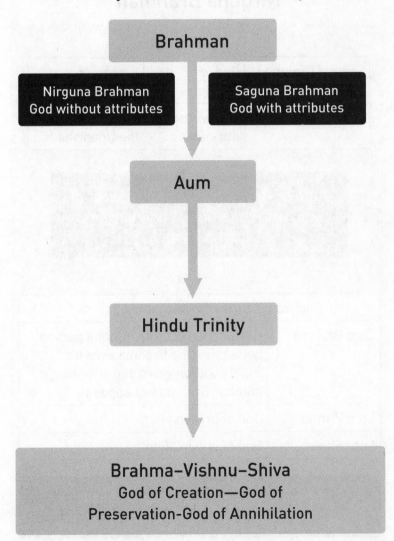

Brahman

Nirguna Brahman
God without attributes

Saguna Brahman
God with attributes

Aum

Hindu Trinity

Brahma–Vishnu–Shiva
God of Creation—God of
Preservation-God of Annihilation

Saguna Brahman and Nirguna Brahman

Saguna Brahman	God with attributes	Viswaroopa
Nirguna Brahman	God without attributes	God described in the Upanishads

Aum or Om is the vibratory aspect of God, who is nameless and formless (nama-roopa).

Godhead is further divided into a Trinity.	
Lord Brahma	God of creation. This is not a person but a title. One Brahma lives for 311.04 trillion years and after that another Brahma will appear.
Lord Vishnu	God of preservation.
Lord Shiva	God of annihilation.

By worshiping any god, you are actually worshiping the only God, Brahman.

If there is only One God, Brahman, why do Hindus worship many gods?

During the time of the Upanishads, when the Hindu **Rishis** said there is only One God, **Brahman**, they found out that **laymen could not understand that concept.**

So they wrote **Ithihasas** (epics) and **Puranas** (mythological stories) filled with many gods, with the idea that **when you worship any god with form, you are actually worshiping the one and only God Brahman,** who is formless and nameless.

It is worth noting that the word 'trinity' does not appear in the sixty-six books of the Holy Bible. It was only at the very first Christian Council at Nicaea (325 CE) that the worship of God in three forms (God the Father, God the Son and God the Holy Ghost) was adopted.

God said:

'Call me by whatever name you like;
worship me in any form you like;
all that worship goes to the One and
Only Supreme Reality.'

Why Do Hindus Worship Idols?

Hindus do not worship idols.

Hindus use idols like everyone else to worship God, who has no name or form

Regarding the image of God, Yajur
Veda 32:3 states:
'Na Tasya Pratima Asti.'
meaning
'There is no image of Him (God).'

GOD is not a man.
GOD is not a woman.
GOD is beyond any human comprehension.
GOD is beyond mind and logic.
So man is forced to use idols to concentrate on a
God who has no form as well as no name.

What is the right way of worship? God with form or God without form?

Lord Krishna said that people can worship him with form as well as without any form.

Lord Krishna said:

'Those who worship me with great faith, I consider them to be perfect. However, **those who worship the impersonal, formless, imperishable Brahman** with proper control of senses also will finally attain me.'

(Bhagavad Gita 12:2,3,4)

Nataraja
(Lord of Dance)

You will see idols of Nataraja, the Lord of Dance in several James Bond movies. You will even see a beautiful Nataraja statue at **CERN**, the **European Center for Research in Particle Physics in Geneva**, symbolizing Shiva's cosmic dance of creation and destruction.

In his article, '**The Dance of Shiva: The Hindu View of Matter in the Light of Modern Physics**', and also in his book Tao of Physics, Fritjof Capra relates Nataraja's dance to modern physics.

Lord Shiva as Nataraja is performing the **Lasya** (creation dance) and the **Tandava** (destruction dance) simultaneously. A small drum in one of his right hands symbolizes the rhythmic creation, the flame of fire in his left hand symbolizes destruction, the dwarf under his feet called Apasmara (also called Tribura Muyalakha) symbolizes overcoming the darkness of ignorance.

What Is 'Aum' or 'Om'?

Aum or Om is the **vibratory aspect of God,** who is nameless and formless.

The whole of creation emerges from Aum (Om).

Anahada Nada

The sound of Aum is called *Anahada Nada* in Sanskrit, meaning 'unstruck sound' or 'sound produced without striking two things together'.

Everything in the whole universe is vibrating at one frequency or another. Even the human body is made of electronic vibrations. The ancient Rishis knew that behind everything is a vibration, and that vibration is the base of all matter.

John 1:1 is similar to a Hymn in the Vedas

'Prajapati vai idam agra asit Tasya vak dvitiya asit Vag vai paramam Brahman.'

'In the beginning was Prajapati, the Brahman—GOD with whom was the Word, and the Word was verily the Supreme Brahman—GOD.'

(Krishna Yajurveda)

John 1:1 states

'In the beginning was the

Word

and the Word was with

God and the Word was God.'

Taxila or Takshashila University

Believe it or not, the **world's first university** was established in **Takshila** or **Taxila** or **Takshashila** (50 km west of present-day Rawalpindi, Pakistan) during **700** BCE.

Taxila flourished from 600 BCE to 500 CE, in the kingdom of Gandhar.

Nalanda University
(500 CE–1300 CE)

Nalanda University, situated in **Magdha (Bihar),** was one of the popular universities existing in India. Nalanda's traditional history dates back to the times of Lord Buddha and the Mahavira, the founder of the Jain religion.

Nalanda University was established during the Gupta Dynasty. Nalanda is known as an ancient center of learning.

Once upon a time, more than 2,000 teachers and 10,000 students from all over the world lived and studied at Nalanda, the first residential international university of the World. They studied more than sixty subjects. Nalanda University's library was one of the biggest libraries of the world at that time.

Nalanda continued to flourish as a center of learning under the Pala Dynasty (750 CE–1174 CE) as well.

The Hindu Empires and Their Pioneers

Maurya Empire
(322–180 BCE)

The **Mauryan Empire** (322 BCE–180 BCE) succeeded the earlier **Magadha Kingdom** to assume power over large parts of India.

The empire came into being when **Chandragupta Maurya** stepped into the vacuum created by **Alexander the Great's** departure from the western borders of India.

In his rise to power, **Chandragupta Maurya** was aided and counselled by his chief minister **Kautilya** (also known as Chanakya), who wrote the book **Arthashastra**, an exposition on statecraft, economic policy and military strategy.

Emperor Ashoka
(304–232 BCE)

Ashoka, called **Ashoka the Great**, was an emperor of the Maurya Dynasty, who ruled almost all of the Indian subcontinent from **304–232** BCE.

He was the grandson of the founder of the Maurya Dynasty, Chandragupta Maurya. Ashoka promoted the spread of Buddhism.

H.G. Wells wrote of Ashoka in his book, *The Outline of History*:

Amidst the tens of thousands of names of monarchs that crowd the columns of history, their majesties and graciousnesses and serenities and royal highnesses and the like, the **name of Ashoka** *shines, and shines, almost alone, a star.*

Gupta Empire
(320–540 CE)

Golden Age of India

The Gupta period (320-540 CE) is the classical age of India, the period during which the norms of Indian literature, art, architecture, and philosophy were established.

The three great kings of Gupta Dynasty are: **Chandragupta I** (320–335 CE), his son **Samudragupta** (335–375 BCE), and his grandson **Chandragupta II/Vikramaditya.** (380–414 BCE)

Aryabhata (476-556 CE), who was a mathematician and astronomer, invented zero.

He lived in Kusuma Pura—near Patalipurta (Patna), then the capital of the Gupta Dynasty, where he composed two works, **Arvabhativa** (c. 499) and **Arvabhatasiddhanta**.

His notable contributions to the world of science and mathematics include:

1. The theory that the earth rotates on its axis,

2. Explanations of the solar and lunar eclipses,

3. Solving of quadratic equations,

4. Place value system with zero, and

5. **Approximation of pi (π).**

Emperor Harsha
(606–647 CE)

Harsha, also known as **Harshavardhana**, was an Indian emperor who ruled North India from 606 to 647 CE.

He was a member of the **Vardhana dynasty** and was the son of **Prabhakarvardhana,** who defeated the Alchon Huna invaders.

According to the Chinese Buddhist traveler **Xuan Zang**, Harsha became a **devout Buddhist** at some point in his life. Harsha is widely believed to be the author of three Sanskrit plays, **Ratnavali, Nagananda** and **Privadarsika**.

Chera Dynasty
(Third century BCE–twelfth century CE)

The **Chera Dynasty** was one of the ancient Tamil dynasties which ruled the states of Kerala and Tamil Nadu in India. The word **Chera** originated from the Tamil word **Cheral** meaning 'slope of a mountain'. The Chera Dynasty was also known as Kerala Putra because of its control over the state of Kerala.

The first Chera ruler was **Perumchottu Utiyan Cheralatan**. Other popular rulers of dynasty were Cheran Senguttuvan, Neduncheralathan and Uthiyan Cheralathan. The true age of the Chera Dynasty is very difficult to ascertain.

The **Sangam poem Shilappadikaram** refers to the rule of the Cheras in the state of Kerala, and their administrative structure. The Chera Dynasty is very popular because of its 'trade' with the Middle East and the Greco-Roman world.

The Chera style of architecture is one of a kind in the Dravidian style of construction. The Thirunelli Temple, the Vadakkunnathan Temples, Kodungallur Bhagavathy Temple and Kandiyur Shiva Temple are some examples.

Shri Adi Sankaracharya
(788–820 CE)

Born at Kaladi, Kerala, **Adi Sankara** was the founder of the Advaita philosophy. He was a versatile genius. Swami Chinmayananda often said, '**Sankara starts where Einstein ends**'.

Just like Jesus Christ, Sankara did not come to destroy, but to fulfill the spiritual vacuum in India during a particular period in Indian history.

Sankaracharya stopped the onslaught of Buddhism on Hindu ideals and restored Hinduism to its past glory. According to him, '**The Brahman alone exists; all the rest is Maya or illusion.** The individual soul (Jeevathman) is Brahman alone and nothing else. People are bound by endless cycles of reincarnations because of their ignorance of the fact that they are the Immortal Soul—Atman.'

Pallava Dynasty
(275–897 CE)

The **Pallava Dynasty** was a very famous South Indian dynasty that ruled a portion of southern India from 275 to 897 CE.

The Pallavas promoted architecture.

Some examples of the magnificent temples they left behind are **Kanchi Kailasanathar Temple**, Kanchipuram, Tamil Nadu (685-705 CE) **Shore Temple** (700-728 CE) and the **monuments at Mahabalipuram** in Tamil Nadu.

Two famous kings of the Pallava Dynasty were **Simhavarman I** (275-300 CE) and **Aparajitavarman** (882-897 CE).

Chalukya Dynasty
(543–753 CE) and (624–1189 CE)

Chalukya Dynasty ruled large parts of South India from 543–753 CE and again from 624 to 1189 CE.

Like the Gupta Empire period is considered the golden age of North India, **the Chalukya Dynasty era is considered the golden age of South India.**

Hinduism was the most prominent religion during the time of the Chalukya Dynasty. During the Chalukya rule, they developed a new style of architecture called '**Chalukyan architecture**'.

Pandyan Dynasty
(Fourth century BCE–sixteenth Century CE)

The Pandyan Dynasty was one of three very popular Tamil dynasties, the other two being Chola and Chera.

Pandya Kings were extremely tolerant. During their time Jainism, Shaivism and Vaishnavism flourished in their kingdom. They excelled in trade and learning. One Pandyan king even sent an emissary to the Roman Emperor Augustus with gifts.

Pandyas ruled from fourth century BCE to sixteenth century CE. Pandyas (1216-1345) entered their golden age under Pandyan kings Maravarman Sundara Pandyan and Jatavarman Sundara Pandyan.

Vijayanagara Empire
(1336–1646 CE)

The **Vijayanagara Empire,** also known as **Karnataka Empire,** was built on the capital city Vijayanagara (Sanskrit: '**City of Victory**').

It was established in 1336 by Harihara I and his brother Bukka Raya I of the Sangama Dynasty. This dynasty lasted until 1646 CE.

The Vijayanagara kings promoted Hinduism, architecture and arts throughout their rule.

Archaeological excavations at Vijayanagara have revealed the empire's power and wealth. Today, the ruins surrounding the capital city Vijayanagara is known as **Hampi,** a world heritage site in Karnataka, India.

Then next time you visit India, you must visit this site of historical importance.

Chola Dynasty
(300s BCE–1279 CE)

Believe it or not, **Chola Dynasty** was one of the most civilized as well as longest ruling dynasties of South India. They left a long-lasting impression with their zeal of building temples. **The Chola period was a golden period for Tamil literature.**

From the inscriptions left by Emperor Ashoka, we have to agree that this dynasty came into existence during the third century BCE. Under the **King Rajaraja** I (985–1018 CE) and his son **King Rajendra Chola** I (1018–1048 CE), Cholas conquered the whole of Tamil Nadu.

The **Cholas built many Shiva temples.** Some Chola temples that have been declared World Heritage Sites by the UNESCO are **Brihadisvara Temple, the temple of Gangaikondacholisvaram** and the **Airavatesvara Temple** at Darasuram, Thanjavur district, Tamil Nadu.

Hinduism and Science

The Time Taken for the Earth to Orbit Around the Sun

The Hindu mathematician, **Bhaskaracharya** (600–680 BCE), in his famous treatise **Surya Siddhanta**, calculated **the time taken for the Earth to orbit the Sun** to nine decimal places (**365.258756484 days**).

Today's accepted measurement is 365.2564 days.

The Fibonacci Pattern of Numbers

Virhanka (700 AD) is the very first Hindu mathematician to describe the **Fibonacci pattern of numbers**.

The **Fibonacci sequence** is a series of numbers where each number is the sum of the two numbers before it. Starting with 0 and 1, the sequence goes 0, 1, 1, 2, 3, 5, 8, 13, 21, 34, 55, 89, 144... and so forth.

Trigonometry

The word **Trigonometry** came from the word **Trikonamiti** which means 'measuring triangular forms' and the study of trigonometric functions flourished during the **Gupta Dynasty**.

Aryabhata (476-556 AD) described trigonometric functions sine and versine in his treatise. Later, the sixth century astronomer **Varahamihira** (505-587 AD) discovered a few basic trigonometric formulas and identities, such as $\sin^2(x) + \cos^2(x) = 1$.

The Decimal System or Hindu-Arabic Numerals

It was indeed the Hindu scholars, during the sixth or seventh century in India, who developed the so-called **Decimal System** or **Hindu-Arabic** numerals, which is a positional numeric system with a set of ten symbols—1, 2, 3, 4, 5, 6, 7, 8, 9, 0

They were introduced to Europe through the writings of Middle Eastern mathematicians, such as **Al-Khwarizmi** and **Al-Kindi**, during the twelfth century.

The system was called Hindu-Arabic because Arabs introduced this **Hindu concept** to the West.

The Pythagoras Theorem

Believe it or not, it was **Baudhāyana**, who lived circa 800 BCE, who discovered the **Pythagoras theorem** (written around 400 BCE).

Baudhāyana described the Pythagoras theorem in his book *Baudhāyana Śulbasutra* (eighth to seventh century BCE). *Baudhayana Sulbasutra* is also one of the oldest books on advanced mathematics.

He is also accredited with calculating the value of pi (π) before Pythagoras.

Gravity

Five hundred years before Newton, Bhaskaracharya in India had already discovered gravity.

We are taught in school that when Sir Isaac Newton (1643–1727 CE) saw an apple falling from a tree, he was inspired to formulate 'The Universal Law of Gravitation'.

But in truth, five hundred years before Sir Isaac Newton, an Indian Mathematician named Bhaskaracharya (1114–1185 CE) had formulated the theory of a gravitational force in his book *Siddhanta Siromani* around 1150 CE.

The word that was used in Sanskrit for gravity is **Gurutvakarshan,** which can be broken down to two words. **Gurutva** and **Aakarshan,** Gurutva means weight and Aakarshan means attraction.

Acharya Charaka
(Father of Medicine)

Born during 300 BCE, **Acharya Charaka** is considered the **true father of Medicine**, since he was the principal contributor to the science of Ayurveda. He wrote the Ayurvedic treatise known as '**Charaka Samhita**'. For the next two hundred years, it was the standout book on medicine in the world.

Acharya believed it is more important to prevent a disease than to treat it. He believed the human body has three **Doshas**, namely **Vata, Pitta** and **Kapha**, and the imbalance of these Doshas creates disease. **Vata** is composed of space and air, **Pitta** of fire and water, and **Kapha** of earth and water.

He also had extensive knowledge of human anatomy, embryology, pharmacology, and blood circulation, as well as about diseases like diabetes and tuberculosis.

Sushruta
(Father of Surgery)

Sushruta, also spelled **Suśruta**, lived during the sixth century BCE and was an ancient Indian surgeon who was known for his pioneering operations on the human body. He wrote a very technical treatise known as *Sushruta-Samhita*, the main source of knowledge about surgery in ancient India.

Amazing it may sound, he had developed very unique ways to dissect a human body. In this treatise, he discussed operations, including rhinoplasty (the repairing or remaking of a nose), removal of a dead fetus from a woman's body, and surgery of the urinary bladder to remove stones or calculi.

The Shape of the Earth

India knew that the Earth is round, long before the Greeks did!

We study in school that 'the concept of a spherical Earth was formulated mainly by Aristotle and Plato around the sixth century BCE'.

But the fact of the matter is, people in India knew Earth is round even before them.

The word **Bhugola** for Earth in Hindu scriptures very clearly points to this fact.

'**Bhu**' means Earth while '**Gola**' means round. Even **Thiruvalluar** (400 BCE), the celebrated Tamil poet and saint, mentioned Earth is round in his *Thirukural.*

Why Do Women Wear a Dot on their Foreheads?

The dot is supposed to represent the meeting point of the eyebrows.

That vital point is called
Anjana Chakra or spiritual eye.

Everyone is supposed to protect that area.
In fact, all saints protect that point with
sandalwood paste.

What Is Namaste?

It is the popular Hindu greeting performed by pressing two hands together and holding them near the heart. The whole act communicates the following to the world:

'You and I are one. I salute and worship the God within you, which is indeed a mirror image of myself'.

Everything about Hinduism is reflected in 'Namaste', since it proclaims to the world that the real 'I' is the immortal soul (Atman) within the body and not the physical body.

Namaste is derived from the Sanskrit language and is a combination of two words, 'Namah' and 'te'. Namah means **'bow'**, **'obeisance'**, **'reverential salutation'** or **'adoration'**, and te means **'to you'**.

Why Do Hindus Worship the Cow?

Hindus respect, honor and adore cows. The cow personifies **'animals'** in general. All animals are sacred in Hinduism.

Mahatma Gandhi said:
'One can measure the greatness of a nation and its moral progress by the way it treats its animals. Cow protection to me is not mere protection of the cow. It means protection of all that lives and is helpless and weak in the world. The cow means the entire subhuman world.'

Sin and Hinduism

Sin means ignorance in Hinduism. Sin is the false belief that one is the perishable body and not the immortal soul within the body and as such Jnana (knowledge) eradicates that ignorance.

Lord Krishna said:
Even if you are the worst sinner in the world,
You can still cross the ocean of sin,
With a bark of wisdom.
(Bhagavad Gita 4:36)

Lord Krishna said:
'As the blazing fire burns wood to ashes,
Arjuna, so does the fire of true knowledge
(Jnana) burn all "karmic debt" to ashes'.
(Bhagavad Gita 4:37)

Heaven and Hell are not Permanent in Hinduism

As far as Lord Krishna is concerned, Heaven and Hell are temporary abodes where the immortal soul resides for a very short period before coming back to Earth to take another body, in order to exhaust all of its karmic debt and attain salvation.

Some religions believe that Heaven and Hell are permanent resting places **for the soul** after death.

Lord Krishna said:
'A man of faith who could not control his mind, who deviated from the spiritual path and failed to attain self-realization and died, will never perish. He will be reborn into a family of pure, pious people after living many years in Heaven and continue his spiritual quest from where he left off in his last life.'

Lord Krishna continued: 'After having enjoyed the vast heavenly realm and with the results of all their pious activities exhausted, they return to this mortal planet (Earth) again.'
(Bhagavad Gita 9:20,21)

What Is Salvation or Moksha or Mukti, According to Hinduism?

Salvation means **realizing** one is indeed the immortal soul or **Atman** within the body and giving up the false belief that one is the perishable body.

That is the reason why **Hindu salvation** is known as **self-realization**. That means **realizing** that one is indeed the self or **Atman** or the immortal soul within the body.

Hindu salvation is also known as **Moksha** or **Mukti,** meaning the liberation or release from the repeated cycles of birth and death known as **Samsara**.

How Can Someone Attain Salvation?

There are four paths or Yogas to attain salvation or self-realization. Most people follow Bhakti Yoga, the path of total surrender to God.

Jnana Yoga	The path of Jnana (knowledge) through introspection and contemplation.
Karma Yoga	The path of selfless service through thoughts and actions.
Raja Yoga	The path of Pranayama and breathing exercises.
Bhakti Yoga	The path of total surrender to God.

Amazing as it may sound, Hindu scriptures have never stated that one has to become a Hindu to attain Moksha or salvation.

Anyone, even atheists, can attain Moksha or salvation as long as they sincerely search after truth.

The best among us will attain salvation within one life.

The worst among us will attain salvation after many lives.

Nobody is denied salvation.

What Is the Hindu Concept of the Soul?

Hindus believe the soul is immortal, and it is called Atman.

Hindu salvation is based on the immortality of the soul.

This belief in the immortality of the soul is unique in eastern religions.

Neither Judaism, nor Christianity nor Islam believes in the immortality of the soul.

Neither the Old Testament nor the New Testament says that the soul is immortal. In the Old Testament, the soul is described by the Hebrew word *nephesh*, which simply means 'a breathing creature'.

Ezekiel 18:4 as well as 18:20 state:
'The soul (*nephesh*) who sins shall die'.
Mathew 10:28 states 'Do not be afraid of those who kill the body but cannot kill the soul. Rather, be afraid of the **One who can destroy both soul and body in hell.'**

Comparing Hindu salvation concepts with salvation concepts from Christianity and Islam is like comparing apples and oranges.

Why so?

Hindu salvation concepts are based on the immortality of the soul. Christianity and Islam do not believe the soul is immortal.

Whenever either of those religions talk about salvation, they mean going to either Heaven or Hell for eternity after one life.

Hindu scriptures state that after death, the soul may go to Heaven or Hell—but that stay is **temporary** and the soul will be reborn again until it exhausts all karmic debt and attains salvation.

You do not have to be a Hindu to attain salvation. Salvation is assured for all, whether someone is a Hindu or not. Even atheists will finally attain salvation.

Nobody Is Lost Forever in Hinduism

Arjuna asked: 'Oh! Krishna, what happens to someone who goes astray from spiritual pursuit, fails to attain salvation and dies?'

Lord Krishna answered:

'**That man will not perish**. He will not meet any destruction in this world nor in the next. **One who has stepped into spiritual pursuit will never be overcome by misfortune.**

'He will be reborn into a family of pure, pious people after living many years in Heaven and continue his spiritual quest where he left off in his last life.'

(Bhagavad Gita 6:36 to 45)

Why Do Hindus Cremate?

Death is never considered as the end of the journey. It is only the end of the perishable body. After that the immortal soul (Atman) takes another body and this cycle of birth and death continues until the person attains self-realization.

Cremation of a person's dead body is therefore supposed to get rid of the perishable body so that the departed soul can move on to another body to continue to deal with 'karmic debt'.

Also, according to Hindu scriptures, a person's body is composed of five elements— earth, fire, water, air and sky, and at death, the body has to go back to the original five elements.

Who Is a True Guru?

Guru actually means God Incarnate in Hinduism, manifesting in a personal form to guide the aspirant.

The word 'Guru' means 'dispeller of darkness' (GU means darkness and RU means that which dispels in Sanskrit).

Bookish knowledge of scriptures does not make someone a Guru. Most people you see who say they are Gurus are merely teachers. A true Guru will be like **Sthita Prajna** (enlightened person), whom Lord Krishna described in chapter 2, verses 54, 55, 56 and 57 of the Bhagavad Gita.

Anyone who does not fit that definition is not a Guru, merely a teacher.

Ultimately, the one and only true Guru is the inner voice within us.

In **one of the Upanishads**, when a disciple asked too many questions, his **Guru** said:

'Nobody knows what is **right**;
Nobody knows what is **wrong**;
Nobody knows what is **Adharma**;
Nobody knows what is **Dharma**:
There is a **deity residing within you**,
Find it and obey its commands.'

What Happens to Us When We Die?

According to Hinduism, the body alone dies.

↓

The immortal soul (**Atman**) within the body never dies, but the path the soul takes is decided by the past actions performed in the former body, which are known as karmas or karmic debts.

↓

After death, depending on the karmic debt, the soul ends up in **Heaven** or **Hell**. After a short stay in either of those places, the soul will take a body again.

↓

Past karmic debts are attached to the soul and they decide what kind of body the soul takes in the next life.

↓

When an individual soul exhausts all its karmic debt, then the person attains salvation or self-realization.

Best and Worst Times to Die

Lord Krishna said: 'Arjuna, let me explain to you the times at which, if yogis depart from the world, they never return.'

(Bhagavad Gita 8:23)

'Those who know God (Brahman) and depart life amidst fire and light and during the bright lunar fortnight or the six months when the sun travels north will not take birth again.'

(Bhagavad Gita 8:24)

'Those who depart amidst smoke and the night and during the dark lunar fortnight or the six months when the sun travels south, will take birth again.'

(Bhagavad Gita 8:25)

In fact, Bhishma waited until the Kurukshetra War ended so that he could depart from Earth during Uttarayana, the six months when the sun travels north.

What Is Yoga?

Yoga is a Sanskrit word meaning **'union with the divine'.**

The Sanskrit word **'Yuj'** means to **'attach to the spirit.'**

Yoga is not a religion.
Yoga is spiritual.

There are **four Yogas** or means to attain salvation or self-realization. They are **Jnana Yoga, Karma Yoga, Raja Yoga, and Bhakti Yoga.**

What Did Patanjali Say about Yoga?

Sage Patanjali wrote in the
Patanjali Yoga Sutra:

'Yoga Chitta Vrithi Nirodha.'

Yoga-Union with the divine

Chitta Vrithi-Mental vibrations

Nirodha-Stoppage

Yoga or self-realization means stoppage of mental activity.

Rishi Vasishta told Lord Rama
in Yoga Vasistha:

'Chit Chalathi Samsare; Nichale
Moksha Muchavatha.'

'When chit (mind) vibrates,
this whole world comes into
existence; when the mind stop
vibrating (stoppage of thoughts),
this whole world is destroyed,
and the person attains salvation.'

Lord Krishna said:
'Arjuna, become a Yogi!'

A Yogi lives like a lotus leaf.

Raindrops falls on a lotus leaf, but the leaf is
not affected by them. Similarly, a Yogi lives in
the world, but the Yogi is unaffected
by the world.

Lord Krishna said:
'Just as the ocean is unaffected by the waters
of innumerable rivers flowing into it; a Yogi
is unaffected by the sensual pleasures of the
positive and negative reactions to actions he
or she takes...'

(Bhaghvad Gita 2:70)

Alexander the Great Meets a Hindu Yogi

When Alexander conquered the northern part of India, he sent **several summons to Yogi Dandini**, which the latter ignored. Alexander, who made great kings shiver, was intrigued.

Finally, Alexander sent his helmsman Onesicritus to praise and give gifts to Yogi Dandini, who refused to accept them. Alexander now threatened Yogi Dandini with death. Yogi Dandini told Onesicritus:

'I want nothing that is Alexander's. Go and tell Alexander that God, the Supreme King, is never the author of insolent wrongs, but is the creator of light, of peace, of water, of the body of man and souls.'

'Alexander is no god, since he must taste death,' continued the **Yogi Dandini** in quiet scorn.

Controlling the **Mind** by Controlling **Breath** Is the Basis of **Pranayama**

Pranayama translates to 'trance induced by the stoppage of all breathing.' It comes from two separate Sanskrit words, *Prāna* (breath) and *Ayama* (stoppage).

Lord Krishna said:

'This royal knowledge, this kingly secret is the purest of all knowledge. It is directly perceivable, easy to practice, and imperishable.'

(Bhagavad Gita 9:2)

Lord Krishna said:

'Some offer inhalation (Apana Vayu) into exhalation (Prana Vayu) and vice versa resulting **in the stoppage of all breathing**. Others, curtailing the eating process, offer the outgoing breath into itself as a sacrifice.'

(Bhagavad Gita 4:29)

Yoga and a Balanced Life

Unlike other religions which demands severe austerities on the part of aspirants, Hindu scriptures advocate for a **well-balanced approach** to dealing with day to day problems and spirituality.

Lord Krishna said:
'Oh! Arjuna, Yoga is not possible for the one who **eats too much**, or who **does not eat at all**; who **sleeps too much**, or who **keeps always awake**.'
(Bhagavad Gita 6:16)

- You do not have **to starve** to become spiritual.
- You do not have to **do severe austerities** in life to become spiritual.
- You do not have **to deny sex** to your spouse to become spiritual.
- You do not have to **wear Kavi or saffron robes** to become spiritual.
- You do not have to **do anything extraordinary** to become spiritual.
- Just live a very natural life.

From time immemorial, Hindu Rishis knew that breathing, thoughts and the mind are very closely connected.

Rishis knew that breath is a very powerful tool to calm the mind. They also knew that **whatever we think, we become.**

- Whenever we get angry;
- Whenever we become emotional;
- Whenever we become sad;
- We have to watch our breathing pattern. It will be erratic and short and rapid.

When we are happy and have sublime thoughts, **the breath is slow and relaxed.** Mental activity also slows down.

So Rishis developed Raja Yogic breathing methods called **Pranayama**, allowing the body and mind to relax and at the same time for the mind to be focused and concentrated.

When Is the Best Time to Study, Pray and Meditate?

It is written in scriptures that we get maximum benefits when we do things during **Brahma Muhurta**, the time between **4 am and 6 am**. Some say it is **3 am to 6 am**.

There are varied opinions about exactly which hours constitute Brahma Murta.

Brahma Muhurta (time of Brahma) is a period (Muhurta) one and a half hours before sunrise—or more precisely, 1 hour 36 minutes (96 minutes) before sunrise.

What Is the Best Way to Manage Stress and Anxiety?

The best way is to practice Hamsa, known as 'baby Pranayama' in Raja Yoga.

What is Hamsa?
Observing exhalation and inhalation without even controlling nostril movements.

'Ha' is the sound of exhalations and 'Sa' is the sound of inhalations. You can do this exercise anywhere at any time. Of course, please do not practice this when driving. The first result is that you will fall asleep. The next result is that you will have free periods of time.

Controlling the Mind

Lord Krishna said:

'One who can control the mind and attain tranquility, to that man "heat" and "cold", "pleasure" and "pain", "honor" and "dishonor" are the same.' (Bhagavad Gita 6:7)

Knowing the power of the mind and its tendency to wander, Lord Krishna asks us to constantly watch it. Like a turtle withdrawing its limbs upon seeing danger, we should withdraw our mind and keep it under the control all the time.

The Four States of Mind or Consciousness

Four states of mind or consciousness are:	
Jagruti	The waking state of mind
Swapna	The dreaming state of mind
Shushupti	The deep sleep state of mind
Turiya	The state beyond mind

When someone enters the **Turiya state,** everything becomes one and the person **transcends duality—** hot and cold, happiness and unhappiness etc.

Lord Krishna gave utmost importance to the mind throughout the Bhagavad Gita, especially in the sixth chapter.

Arjuna said:

'Oh Krishna, since the mind is unsteady, turbulent, obstinate and very strong, controlling the mind is more difficult than controlling the wind.'

Lord Krishna answered:

'Undoubtedly Arjuna, the mind is restless and very difficult to control, but it can be controlled by constant practice and by detachment.'

Bhagavad Gita 6:33, 34 and 35

Hindu scriptures state, 'Any thought once made, circles around us like bees around a flower.'

All thoughts count, however insignificant you may think they are. **A thought never dies**. It may lose its power or strength in time. But it never dies completely.

If you repeatedly think about the same thing, then that thought will become a power source.

If you repeatedly think that you will get into an accident, then you will get into an accident. Your very powerful negative thoughts will get you into that accident.

If you develop thoughts of prosperity, you will change your life dramatically, even if you are a pauper at present.

According to Hindu scriptures, **'A person who suffers from guilty conscience cannot be saved even by God.'** No Hindu should ever say **'I am a sinner'** or dwell on negative thoughts.

What Does God Want of Us?

God is interested only in our sincere devotion. Any prayer in any language in very simple words will do.

Lord Krishna said:

'If one offers Me with love and devotion a leaf, a flower, a fruit or water, I will accept it.'
(Bhagavad Gita 9:26)

We do not need to chant Mantras or have knowledge of rituals to worship God.
Of course that does not mean Mantras are not important. They do help.

Surrender All Actions to God and Act Selflessly

Lord Krishna said:

'Arjuna, one who takes selfless actions, one who performs his duty without attachment, surrendering his actions to God, is not stained or infected by karmic debt, just as the lotus leaf is untouched by water.'

(Bhagavad Gita 5:10)

Lord Krishna is telling us that we will derive no karmic debt if we act selflessly (Nishkama Karma) and surrender our actions to God.

What Does It Mean to Surrender to God?

Lord Krishna said:
'Arjuna, abandon all Dharma (duties)
and just surrender unto me (the will of God).
I shall deliver you from all bonds of karma.
Do not fear.'

(Bhagavad Gita 18:66)

Surrendering does not mean to sit idle, but to
allow God to work through us, becoming an
instrument of God.

To surrender ourselves to God means
to allow God to work through us or
follow our inner voice.

What Happens When We Pray?

First Stage: All devotees start by praying to a personal God with name and form.

Second Stage: As the devotee matures spiritually, that personal God will transform to light in the mind of the devotee.

Third Stage: That light will transform to nothing or void in the devotee's mind.

Fourth Stage: Finally the devotee will realize he or she is one with God. At that time the devotee will say 'Ah Btehmasmi (I am God).' All mystics around the globe have said this.

Searching after God

Thousands of years ago, Rishis wrote: Searching after God, is like a pinch of salt trying the find the bottom of the ocean.

The moment the pinch of salt touches the surface of the ocean, it becomes part and parcel of the ocean...

Similarly, a person who searches after God, will become part and parcel of God, or the limited ego will become the unlimited God.

What Is the Law of Karma?

Karma is all that a person has done, is doing, and will do in future. Karma is not the same as punishment or reward.

Karma also means the cycle of cause and effect.

According to the theory of karma, whatever happens to a person happens because he or she caused it with his or her actions in this life or in previous lives.

Karma is an important part of Hinduism, Jainism, Buddhism and Sikhism.

According to karma theory, **good actions as well as good thoughts** bring forth good karmic results and **bad actions as well as bad thoughts** bring forth bad karmic results. Thus one's thoughts and actions dictate one's happiness and unhappiness.

Beware of Karma

- It will always come back and bite you.

- Life is indeed an echo chamber or a boomerang.

- Whatever we think or do will always come back to us.

- There is no such thing as an action without results.

- Whatever we sow, we will eventually reap.

- Sometimes it may not happen in this life, but believe me, it will happen in future lives.

Nishkama Karma

One of the best methods to attain
Moksha or salvation or self realization
is to take selfless actions—Nishkama Karma.

Lord Krishna said:
'Arjuna, **one who does selfless actions**, one
who performs his duty without attachment,
**surrendering his actions to God, is not
stained or infected by karmic debt**, as the
lotus leaf is untouched by water.'

(Bhagavad Gita 5:10)

Both Lord Krishna as well as Jesus Christ are
telling us that we **should do things without
expecting any compliments or rewards.** The
moment we look forward to any reward, our
action becomes tainted and we incur
karmic debt.

What Is Samsara?

Samsara is the repeated cycle of birth, life, death and reincarnation due to the consequences of one's actions in the past, present, and future.

Hinduism, Jainism, Buddhism, Sikhism and even Taoism believe in Samsara.

What Is Reincarnation?

The word reincarnate means to **'re-enter in the flesh.'**

Hindus believe the soul within the body is immortal, calling it **Atman**. Just like a man discards his old clothes for new ones, so too the immortal soul within the body leaves the worn-out body and enters a new body at the time of death.

The immortal soul **migrates from body to body** until the person exhausts all of his or her karmic debt.
At that time the person will attain **Moksha** or salvation.

Monogamy and Hinduism

Hindus practice monogamy. Child marriages among Hindus in India were stopped by the **Sharda Act** (1929) under the British.

The Hindu Marriage Act (1955) strictly **prohibits Hindus from practicing polygamy**, even though polygamy and polyandry were prevalent in ancient India.

In India, **marriages are not between two people**, but between two families, and that is the reason why **arranged marriages** are still common in India.

Abortion and Hinduism

Abortion is known as **garha batta** (womb killing) and **bhroona hathya** (killing the undeveloped soul).

From time immemorial, Hindus consider children as gifts from God. In his code, Manu forbids **abortion**.

One of the worst acts described in the scriptures is **Sishu Hatya**, meaning destruction of the unborn foetus.

There are prayers in the Rig Veda to guard a growing embryo. The only time abortion is allowed is when the fetus is known to be defective, as per the **Sushruta Samhita**, the Hindu Ayurvedic book.

What Are Ashramas and Ashrama Dharmas?

According to Hindu scriptures, human life is believed to comprise four stages based on physical and mental development.

Stage	Age	Recommended Activities
Brahmacharya	8 to 18	Student life. No sex. Acquiring knowledge in scriptures and other academic teachings.
Grahasthya	18 to 40	Married life. Taking care of wife and children. A person is supposed to take care of all his desires such as Artha (money) and Kama (sexual desires) during this stage.
Vanaprastha	40 to 68	After the completion of one's householder duties, one gradually withdraws from the world, freely shares wisdom with others, and prepares for the complete renunciation of the final stage.
Sanyasa	68 to death	One completely withdraws from the world and starts dedicating himself to spiritual pursuits, seeking self-realization (freedom from the cycle of rebirth).

Every human being is supposed to go through these four stages in life, called 'Ashramas', for smooth functioning of life.

According to Hindu scriptures, nobody can bypass any of the 'Ashramas.'

Even Adi Sankara as well as Suka Maharishi **were forced** to not jump from Brahmacharya to Vanaprastha bypassing Grahasthya Ashrama, even though they attempted to bypass it.

The sex abuse problems occurring in some religious institutions today are due to priests bypassing **Grahasthya Ashrama (married life)**.

Celibacy cannot be forced on anyone.

Purusharthas

Four aspects of life, called **Purusharthas**, were developed by Rishis to help a human being slowly mature from **materialism** to **spirituality**.

Purusharthas do not demand a life of self-negation, but a very balanced approach to life.

1. Dharma (duty, righteousness)
2. Artha (wealth)
3. Kama (desire, passion) and
4. Moksha (salvation or liberation)

Who Am I?

This is one of the most thought-provoking questions a person will have in his or her life.

Adi Sankara answered this question in his popular six-stanza prayer known as the 'Atmashatkam' or 'Nirvanashatkam'.
It was written around 788–820 CE.

I am not the body. I am the God within.
I am the Atman, the immortal soul,
which is indeed God.

What Is the Meaning of 'Neti-Neti'?

Neti-Neti means
'not this-not this' in Sanskrit.

This statement answers the most
important question, 'Who Am I?'
(Brihadaranyaka Upanishad 2:3:6)

With the aid of this statement, a person
negates the identification of himself or herself
as the perishable material body and comes
to the realization that he or she is indeed the
immortal soul within the body (Atman), which
is the mirror image of God.

Through this inquiry, a devotee will finally
realize that he or she is indeed the immortal
soul within the body and will say
Aham Brahmasmi (I am God).

Yugas

In Hinduism, **time** is divided in to periods called Yugas. According to Hindu cosmology, the whole universe is created and destroyed within the time period of four Yugas lasting 4,320,000 years.

Like the Earth goes through seasons such as Summer, Spring, Winter and Autumn, each Yuga involves gradual changes in which the Earth and the consciousness of mankind go from a golden age to a complete dark age.

The four Yugas are as follows:

Yugas	Time period	Size of each Yuga
Krita or Satya Yuga	1,728,000 years	(Four times that of Kali Yuga)
Treta Yuga	1,296,000 years	(Thrice that of Kali Yuga)
Dvapara Yuga	864,000 years	(Twice that of Kali Yuga)
Kali Yuga	432,000 years	

One Maha Yuga	Four Yugas	4,320,000 years
One Kalpa	1,000 Maha Yugas	4,320,000,000 years.
One day of Brahma	One Kalpa	4,320,000,000 years.
One night of Brahma	One Kalpa	4,320,000,000 years.
One complete day of Brahma	Two Kalpas	8,640,000,000 years

Is Lord Brahma Immortal?

The life span of Lord Brahma is
311.04 trillion human years.

After that another
Lord Brahma will come.

Even Lord Brahma will not live forever.

Lord Brahma, unlike Lord Vishnu and
Lord Shiva, is not a person. It is a title.

When Did Kali Yuga Start?

Around 3102 BCE.

It began after King Pareekshit died of the serpent Tashaka's bite.

Some say it started after Lord Krishna left Earth and went back to Vaikuntha.

Astronomer and mathematician Aryabhata wrote in the Aryabhatiya (499 CE) that Kali Yuga began in 3102 BCE.

What Is Maya?

Maya means 'illusion'. The word Maya is derived from the Sanskrit root words 'ma' meaning not and 'ya' meaning that. So the meaning of Maya is 'that which is not'.

Lord Krishna said that the whole creation is his **Leela** (divine child's play) and came from his **Maya** (illusion).

Just like the 'on' and 'off' switches on a computer can create thousands of illusions for all of us, through Maya, God is recreating the entire illusion of existence over and over again.

What message is Lord Krishna conveying to us by saying everything is Maya or Illusion?

Lord Krishna is telling us that pursuing happiness in the material world is like pursuing the mirage of an oasis in the desert, since one will never find water in a desert.

Similarly, the material world provides no real happiness, and exists only as an elusive dream.

Lord Krishna is telling us that only by realizing one is the immortal soul (Atman) within the body, can one transcend Maya (illusion).

That is the reason why Hindu salvation is known as self-realization. That means realizing that one is the immortal soul or Atman within and not the perishable material body (Maya).

That is also the reason why our scriptures say that sin is the ignorance of the truth—that one is the Immortal Soul, Atman—and Jnana (knowledge) eradicates that ignorance.

Athithi Devo Bhava

These are the most enchanting words of greeting from the *Taittiriva Upanishad*.

Mathru devo bhava,
(treat your mother as God)
pithru devo bhava.
(treat your father as God)
acharya devo bhava,
(treat your guru as God)
athithi devo bhava.
(treat your guest as God)

What Is Kundalini Power?

The term **Kundalini** or 'serpent power' is used to refer to the vital force or energy that is within us.

It is represented as a serpent coiled around the first **Chakra** or **root Chakra** or **Muladhara Chakra** at the base of the spine.

The Seven Chakras (Energy Centres)

1. Muladhara Chakra
Base of the spine—four petals—controls smell

2. Swadisthana Chakra
Base or opposite of the genitals—
six petals—controls taste

3. Manipura Chakra
Opposite to the navel—ten petals—
controls sight

4. Anahata Chakra
Opposite to the heart—twelve petals—
controls touch

5. Visudha Chakra
Located at the medulla oblongata—
sixteen petals—controls hearing

6. Ajna Chakra
Located between the eyebrows—two—
petals—controls mind

7. Sahasrara Chakra
At the top of the head—1,000 petals—centre of
Cosmic Consciousness

Five Koshas and Atman

Long before the birth of medical science, Rishis knew that the human body consists of five layers called Koshas, ranging from the dense physical body to the more subtle levels of emotions, mind, and spirit.

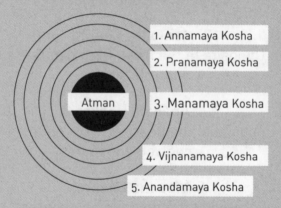

1. Annamaya Kosha
2. Pranamaya Kosha

Atman

3. Manamaya Kosha

4. Vijnanamaya Kosha

5. Anandamaya Kosha

These five sheaths are independent of the **Atman** (the immortal soul).

Hindu temples are constructed to represent the five **Koshas** of the human body, and the place where we install the deity is called **Garbha Griha**.

Mudras

'Mudra' is a Sanskrit word meaning a symbolic hand gesture that has the power of producing happiness.

You can create different Mudras with your hands. It's a very common practice in the East, and they are used by spiritual leaders in both Hinduism and Buddhism. In the modern era, yogis and other meditation practitioners use Mudras.

The important Mudras are: Abhaya, Matsya, Gyan, Vayu, Agni, Prithvi, Varuna, Shoonya, Surya, and Prana. Mudras have been an integral part of many Hindu and Buddhist rituals.

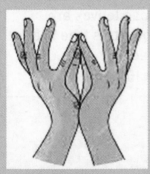
Padma Mudra

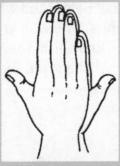
Matsa Mudra

Abhaya Mudra

The Upside Down Asvattha Tree

In the fifteenth chapter of the
Bhagavad Gita, called **Purushottama Yoga**,
Lord Krishna describes the upside down
Asvattha tree of **Samsara** with its roots
above and branches below. According to him,
this tree should be chopped with the 'axe of
detachment', to attain salvation.

Lord Krishna said:
'It is said that there is an imperishable
Asvattha tree with its roots above and
branches below and whose leaves are
Vedic hymns. One who knows this tree is a
knower of the Vedas.'
(Bhagavad Gita 15:1)

Mantras

'Asatoma Sadgamaya' is known as the Shanti mantra (mantra of peace). It is taken from the Brihadaranyaka Upanishad (1:3:28).

Asato mā sadgamaya
Tamasomā jyotir gamaya
Mrityormāamritam gamaya
Om śhānti śhāntih

–Brihadaranyaka Upanishad 1:3:28

'Lead me from the unreal to the real; lead me from darkness to light; lead me from death to immortality. Aum... peace, peace, peace.'

'Lokah Samasta Sukhino Bhavantu'

May all (Samasta) the world (Lokah)
become (Bhavantu) happy (Sukhino).

This mantra came from the realization
that **everything in the universe is connected
to one another** and all of us are one universal
mind, one energy.

After all, we are just stardust!

Satyameva Jayate

'Satyameva Jayate' or 'truth alone triumphs' is a mantra from the Mundaka Upanishad (3:1:6)

'Satyameva Jayate' has been adopted as the national motto of the Indian Republic. It is inscribed in the script at the base of the national emblem as well as on **all denominations of Indian currency.**

The literal translation of the whole verse is:

'Truth alone triumphs, not falsehood. Through truth, the divine path is spread out by which the sages, whose desires have been completely fulfilled, reach to where there is the supreme treasure of Truth.'

Gayatri Mantra

The **Gayatri mantra**, also known as the **Savitri mantra**, is a highly revered mantra from the Rig Veda, dedicated to Savitr, the sun deity, and first recited by **Rishi Vishwamitra**.

It is not true that women cannot chant the Gayatri mantra. Nowhere is it written that women cannot chant the Gayatri Mantra.

'Aum Bhuh Bhuvah Svah Tat Savitur Varenyam Bhargo Devasya Dheemahi Dhiyo Yo Nah Prachodayat'

–Rig Veda (10:16:3)

'We meditate on that most adored Supreme Lord, the creator, whose effulgence (divine light) illumines all realms (physical, mental and spiritual) of life. May this divine light illuminate our intellect.'

Kumbha Mela Festival
(Celebration of the Pot)

The Kumbha Mela Festival is the greatest Hindu pilgrim, age festival, and takes place once in three years. According to the Guinness Book of World Records, this festival is **the largest religious gathering of people on earth.**

It is a riverside religious festival that rotates between four places: **Allahabad** (on the banks of the Ganges, the Yamuna and the mythical Saraswati), **Haridwar** (Ganges), **Ujjain** (Sipra) and **Nasik** (Godavari). The festival that is held in Allahabad every twelve years is known as **Maha Kumbha Mela.**

The Sanskrit term Kumbha Mela means 'celebration of the pot.' The mythological story behind the Kumbha (pot) Mela (celebration) is that once, the **Devatas** (celestial beings in heaven) and **demons** fought over a **pot** (kumbha) **containing Amrita, the elixir of immortality,** produced by their joint churning of the milky ocean. During the struggle, drops of the Amrita fell on four earthly sites and those sites, became very important to Hindus. **Kumbha Mela** is the celebration of that incident.

What Is the Significance of Number 9 in Hinduism?

1	108 Upanishads	(1+0+8=9)
2	18 chapters of Bhagavad Gita	(1+8=9)
3	18 chapters of Mahabharata	(1+8=9)
4	18 Major Puranas	(1+8=9)
5	Kali Yuga- 432,000 years	(4+3+2=9)
6	Dvapara Yuga- 864,000 years	(8+6+4=9)
7	Treta Yuga-1,296,000 years	(1+2+9+6=9)
8	Satya Yuga- 1,728,000 years	(1+7+2+8=9)
9	Kalpa Yuga- 432,000,000 years	(4+3+2=9)
10	9 forms of Bhakti (devotion)	
11	9 planets (Navagraha)	
12	Human body is supposed to have 9 gates	
13	Goddess Durga is worshiped for 9 days	
14	108 beads in Japa Mala	(1+0+8=9)

Pancha Maha Bhoota

According to Ayurveda, the whole of creation is made of **Pancha Maha Bhoota** or five elements. These elements are: **Prithvi** (earth), **Apas** or **Jal** (water), **Agni** or **Tejas** (fire), **Vayu** (air), and **Aakash** (ether).

However, **Acharya Charaka**, the father of medicine, did not accept Aakash (ether or space) as a basic element since it is not perceptible like the other four elements. So in his Ayurvedic treatise, known as *Charaka Samhita* he left out Aakash (ether or space).

According to the **Vaisheshika school**, creation is made of nine elements. Apart from the five **Pancha Maha Bhoota**, there are an additional four elements, including **Kala** (time), **Dik** (space), **Atman** (self) and **Manas** (mind).

Food and Hinduism

There are three types of food. **Sattvic food** consists of fruits, vegetables, whole grains, nuts, milk, spices such as basil, coriander, ginger etc. **Rajasic foods** consists of coffee, tea, cola drinks, and overly spicy and salty food. According to Ayurveda, **any rotten food is Tamasic.** These foods include meat, fish, onions, garlic, mushrooms, and alcohol.

Lord Krishna said:
'Arjuna, people consume three types
of food, according to the three Gunas
(three modes of nature).'
(Bhagavad Gita 17:7)

1	Sattvic (17:8)	Foods that promote health, life and strength
2	Rajastic (17:9)	Foods that are excessively bitter, sour, salty and dry
3	Tamasic (17:10)	Foods that are stale, tasteless, decomposed, rotten and left over

Fasting and Hinduism

Hindus fast not out of obligation or as a sacrifice to God, **but to purify the body and mind**. The Manusmriti has elaborate rules and regulations for fasting on specific occasions. There are different forms of fasting in Hinduism, some of which are extremely strict, and some of which are not.

Unlike in some other religions, there is no extreme fasting in Hinduism. There are several periods of fasting. Hindus fast to please different deities. They fast on **Purnima** (full moon day) every month. They also fast during **Ekadashi**, which happens twice a month, on the eleventh day of each ascending and descending moon. Apart from this, they also fast during festivals like Navaratri (the nine nights associated with mother goddess Durga), Shivaratri (associated with Lord Shiva), and *Karwa Chauth* (married women fasting for the good of husband and family).

Homosexuality and Hinduism

Homosexuality is generally considered a taboo subject in India and as such you will seldom see anyone discussing about that in real life or in books.

First and foremost, sex was never considered as a taboo in Hindu culture, and we never condemned sex like other cultures did. We promoted healthy sex between men and women through books like *Kama Sutra.*

Narada Smriti and **Manu Smriti** forbid **homosexuality** (maithuna pumsi). Sage Manu wrote in Manusmriti: 'Dwijas should not engage in homosexuality.' (Dwijas are Brahmanas, Kshatriyas and Vaisyas.)

Hindu scriptures discuss a third sex or third gender— Tritiya-prakriti (literally, 'third nature') or **Napumsaka** (neither male or female). This category includes a wide range of people with mixed male and female natures such as effeminate males, masculine females, transgender people, transsexual people, the intersexed, and so on. The most well-known third-gender group in India is called Hijra, and they live in North India.

Suttee or Sati

Hindu scriptures do not mention **Sati**, the most horrendous act of widows killing themselves by jumping into the funeral pyres of their dead husbands—sometimes willfully and sometimes by being forced by others.

The Suicide of Sati, the consort of Lord Shiva, or the **suicide of queen Madri** in the Mahabharata, or the **suicide of the 16,000 wives of Lord Krishna** in Srimad Bhagavata Purana, have nothing to do with Sati or Suttee.

Then where did Sati come from?
Sati had its roots in Greece. Pyre sacrifices similar to Sati were prevalent among Germans, Slavs and other races besides Greeks. The practice of Sati came to India through the Kushans during 1 CE.

Who practised Sati in India?
It was the Rajputs, a warrior tribe who were descendants of the Kushans and fanatical and extremely monogamous Hindus, who practiced Suttee.

What happened to Sati?
In 1829, the British government in India outlawed Sati or Suttee as a criminal offense. Sati or Suttee was never practised in South India. Copycats appear now and then, but the **vast majority of Hindus have nothing to do with Sati or Suttee.**

The Caste System

The Varna or 'Caste' system started as a division of labour for the smooth functioning of society during Rig Vedic times. It had nothing to do with a person's birth.

The English word 'caste' derives from the Spanish/Portuguese 'casta'. No such word exists in the Hindu scriptures.

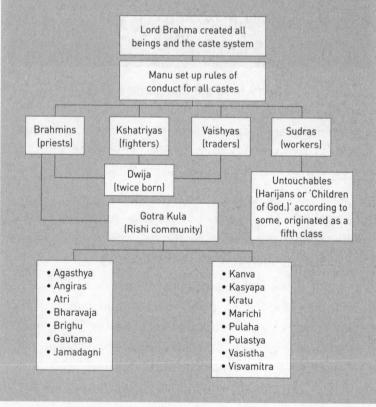

Lord Krishna very clearly stated that **Varna or caste is not decided by birth** but by the aptitudes and professional interests of a person.

Lord Krishna said:

'According to people's ingrained aptitudes (Gunas) and professional interests, I created the four divisions called Varna or caste of human society. Even though I am the author of the caste system, one should know that I do nothing and I am eternal.'

(Bhagavad Gita 4:13)

According to the Mahabharata, caste is not decided by birth but by character alone.

In the epic Mahabharata, in a very popular dialogue between Yaksha and Dharmaputra, Yaksha tells Dharmaputra:

'A man does not become a Brahmin by the mere fact of his birth, not even by the acquisition of Vedic scholarship; it is good character alone that can make one a Brahmin.

He will be worse than a Shudra if his conduct is not in conformity with the rules of good behavior.'

Lord Krishna further said about Varna or Caste:

'A learned and enlightened person sees with equal vision a learned Brahmin, an outcast, a cow, an elephant, or a dog.'

(Bhagavad Gita 5:18)

Adi Sankara, even though he was a Brahmin, condemned caste and meaningless rituals as foolish. He said every human being takes birth as a Shudra. Only by education and upbringing does he or she becomes a twice born (Dwija).

The Swastika

The Swastika ('luck' or 'well-being' in Sanskrit) is a symbol of Hinduism. It is an auspicious symbol for Hindus, Buddhists, and Jains. Hindus and Jains draw Swastika marks on books, doors, offerings, etc.

The Swastika figure is in the form of a Greek cross with the ends of the arms bent at right angles. **The right-handed Swastika moves in a clockwise direction and the left-handed Swastika moves in a counterclockwise direction.**

This symbol creates an impression of perpetual motion. The right-handed Swastika is considered a solar symbol or a fire symbol. The left-handed Swastika is sometimes considered a symbol of the mother goddess Kali.

Usually all Swastikas are white on a black background, but during the Nazi regime, a black left-handed Swastika or 'Hakenkreuz' became the characteristic emblem of the Nazi Party.

Why Don't Hindus Actively Convert Others to Their Religion?

Because Hinduism is a culture, a way of life, not an organized religion like Islam or Christianity.

Hinduism is like physics or chemistry or mathematics. It is a science and not a religion. It is man's relentless search after truth and it does not put any barriers before truth. You even have the right to search for truth in other religious scriptures.

Rishis were not preachers. They were scientists of the past era. They even allowed atheists to debate them. Like modern scientists, they were interested in finding truth and nothing else.

There is no need for Hindus to forcibly convert others to Hinduism, since when people search after truth, they will automatically end up in Hinduism.

If you educate others about Hindu culture, they will **automatically fall in love with Hinduism.** Thus, we do not have to force others to become Hindus.

What Makes Hinduism Unique and Great?

The greatness of Hinduism can be summarized in a few words: 'Freedom of thoughts and actions.'

Nobody is killed or crucified for challenging the Vedas or any other scriptures. In fact, Hindus worship Lord Buddha, who challenged the authority of the Vedas and the Hindu form of worship.

Even an atheist has the right to condemn Hinduism in public and still proudly say that he or she is a Hindu.

Why Is Hinduism So Complex and Difficult to Understand?

All religions are the result of the works of thousands of thinkers over thousands of years. Hinduism and Judaism are cultures, and they are the mothers of all religions.

Hinduism, for its part, never had any house cleaning in its history, like other religions did.

Since Hinduism never tossed anything away, in it you will see very primitive ideas as well as very advanced thoughts.

What Was India's Original Name?

The name **Bharat** for **India** came from the name of **Bharat Chakravarti**, an emperor of the land. He was born **as the son of King Dushyanta and Shakuntala** during the seventh incarnation of Manu.

Believe it or not, there is another Bharat, who was born as the **son of Lord Rishabha**, the very first Thirthankara of Jainism, during the very first incarnation of Manu.

After independence from the British, on September 18, 1949, the Constituent Assembly deliberated upon various names for the yet-to-be-born Indian nation—'Bharat', 'Hindustan', 'Bharatbhumi', 'Bharatvarsha'. Ultimately, Article 1 (1) of the Constitution of India became the official and the only provision on the naming of the nation, stating, '**India, that is Bharat, shall be a Union of States.**'

Famous Sons of India

Mahatma Gandhi
(1869–1948 CE)

Mohandas Karamchand Gandhi, father of the Indian nation, was the leader of the Indian independence movement against British rule. The title **Mahatma** was first given to him in 1914 in South Africa. In India, he is also called **Bapu**.

Engaging in non-violent civil disobedience, **Mahatma Gandhi** led India to independence and inspired movements for civil rights and freedom across the world.

When Gandhiji said: 'I wear only clothes I make' he meant that he literally made the clothes that he wore. No other leader or politician anywhere in this world can say that, or act like him. That may be reason why Albert Einstein said about Gandhiji: 'Generations to come will scarce believe that such a one as this ever in flesh and blood walked upon this Earth.'

Swami Vivekananda
(1863–1902 CE)

Swami Vivekananda, whose original name was **Narendranath Datta,** was born in Bengal, India on 12 January 1863. He was the chief disciple of the great mystic Sri Ramakrishna. Vivekananda was the major force in the revival of Hinduism in India. He introduced Vedanta and Yoga to the western world.

He is well known for his speech at the Parliament of World Religions in Chicago in 1863. Swami Vivekananda conducted hundreds of public and private lectures and classes in many parts of the United States, England, and Europe, teaching Westerners all about Vedanta as well as Yoga. His birthday is celebrated in India as National Youth Day.

Addressing the Parliament of religions on 11 September, 1893 at Chicago Swami Vivekananda said:

'...I am proud to belong to a religion which has taught the world both tolerance and universal acceptance. We believe not only in universal toleration, but we accept all religions as true. I am proud to belong to a nation which has sheltered the persecuted and the refugees of all religions and all nations of the Earth...'

Pandit Jawaharlal Nehru
(1889–1964 CE)

Born as the son of Motilal Nehru (1861–1931 CE), a self-made wealthy barrister who belonged to the Kashmiri Pandit Brahmin community, Pandit Nehru had all kinds of privileges during childhood. His mother, Swaruprani Thussu (1868–1938 CE) also came from a well-known Kashmiri Brahmin family.

But he did not care much for his privileged life and became a freedom fighter. He was twice elected as the president of the Indian National Congress in 1919 and 1928. Finally, he emerged as an eminent leader of the Indian Independent movement along with Mahatma Gandhi. Later he became the first Prime Minister of India from 1947 until his death in 1964.

Of all the things Pandit Nehru has done as the Prime Minister of India, one that stands out is the establishment of the India Institutes of Technology (IITs). On the recommendation of the N.R. Sarkar Committee Report (1946), the first Indian Institute of Technology was established in Kharagpur in May 1950. Within a decade, four more IITs were established in (then) Bombay, Madras, Kanpur, and Delhi to meet the growing technological demands of the planned economy.

Generations to come should pay thanks to Pandit Nehru, for his vision and for being the chief architect behind the creation of the IITs.

Sardar Vallabhbhai Patel
(1875–1950 CE)

Sardar Vallabhbhai Patel was the first Deputy Prime Minister of India. Just like Pandit Nehru, he was also a freedom fighter as well as a very senior member of the Indian National Congress. He played a leading role during India's independence struggle.

Along with Mr V.P. Menon of Kerala, Sardar Vallabhbhai Patel is well known for the integration of India, bringing all the feuding states together under the Indian Government after Independence. He is rightly called the 'Unifier of India.' Threatening military force, Sardar Patel persuaded almost every state to accede to India. The only ruler he had to literally force to concede was the Nizam of Hyderabad, Mir Osman Ali Khan. Mr Patel's commitment to national integration in the newly independent country also earned him another deserving title, 'Iron Man of India'.

In 2014, the Government of India introduced a commemoration of Patel, held annually on his birthday, October 31, and known as Rashtriya Ekta Diwas (National Unity Day).

V.P. Menon
(1894–1966 CE)

Rao Bahadur Vappala Pangunni Menon was an Indian civil servant who played a vital role during the partition of India and the integration of independent India, in the period between 1945–1950.

Even though the world and history recognizes Sardar Patel as the true architect of the integration of all states in India, the genius behind Mr Patel's actions was none other than V.P. Menon. He was also a CIS (Companion of the Order of the Star of India) and a CIE (Companion of the Order of the Indian Empire), rewards for outstanding achievements founded by King George V and Queen Victoria respectively.

Born and brought up in Kerala, Mr Menon achieved a junior post in the Indian Civil Service. By working tirelessly, Menon rose through the ranks and in 1946, he was appointed as the Political Reforms Commissioner to the British Viceroy, Lord Louis Mountbatten.

Even though he could have become the Prime Minister of India, Mr Menon lived a very humble life as a civil servant in the Indian Government.

What Does Hinduism
Say about How We Should Sleep?

According to Vastu Shastra (the ancient Indian science of harmony and prosperous living) and Ayurveda, the best and healthiest way to sleep is to do so in the east-west direction, with the head facing east and legs facing west.

According to both scriptures, our sleep positions play a vital role in absorbing the energy waves that come towards us. This increases concentration and memory. Also, it attracts positivity and keeps you healthy.

According to science, Earth is a magnet and we humans have a natural magnetic compass in our bodies. The North Pole is considered as a source of negative energy and the South Pole is a source of positive energy. So, if you sleep with your head towards the north, your tired brain gets access to negative energy, which will result in developing insomnia, high blood pressure and high cholesterol.

Did Jesus Visit India?

It is speculated that Jesus was disheartened by the state of Jewish society when he was young. So at the early age of thirteen, Jesus abandoned Jerusalem and made a pilgrimage to India by caravan to improve and perfect himself with the philosophy and ideals of Hinduism as well as the teachings of Lord Buddha.

According to this theory, he landed in Punjab and reached the Puri Jagannathan Temple, where he studied the Vedas and the Upanishads under the Brahmin priests. He even spent some years near Nalanda, the ancient Hindu university. Then he left for Tibet to study under Tibetan Buddhist monks, and returned to Jerusalem at the age of 29.

Many suspect statements by Jesus like 'show your right cheek' when the rest of the Middle-East was preaching 'an eye for an eye', came from the Buddhist influence of compassion and humility.

According to a Russian war correspondent, Nicolas Notovitch (1887), there is a document in one of the monasteries in Tibet called 'Life of Saint Issa, Best of the Sons of Men'—Isa being the Arabic name of Jesus in Islam. Notovitch's story, with a translated text of the 'Life of Saint Issa', was published in French in 1894 as *La vie inconnue de Jesus Christ (The Unknown Life of Jesus Christ)*. Many modern day scholars consider this a hoax.

The Gnostic Gospels

The Gnostic Gospels are a set of gospels which were expunged or deleted from the Holy Bible, since the contents of those gospels are like what is written in the Upanishads.

The **Gnostic Gospels** consist of about fifty-two ancient texts based upon the teachings of several spiritual leaders, written from the second to the fourth century CE.

The Gospel of Mary Magdalene reads:
'Take care that no one deceives you by saying "Look over here. Look over here"...for the true child of humanity is within you. Follow it. For those who seek it will find it.'

In the Gospel of Thomas, Jesus said:
'Whoever drinks from my mouth will become like me; myself shall become that person, and the hidden things will be revealed to him.'

The Origin of Christianity in India

Believe it or not, Christianity came to India through Apostle Thomas.

Apostle Thomas (Doubting Thomas) came to Muziris on the Kerala coast in 52 AD, which is in present-day Pattanam, Kerala.

According to a very ancient Syriac work, *The Acts of Thomas*, Apostle Thomas took a boat to Malabar, Kerala in 52 CE and reached a place very close to Cochin, Kerala and later established churches all over Kerala. He even traveled to China and finally died at Mylapore, Madras in 72 CE.

'Love Thy Enemy'

The love that Jesus Christ was propagating is beyond all human emotions. It is very spiritual.

Hindu scriptures state,
'By sending powerful thoughts of love to your enemy, you will become a fortress of love.'

Your enemy will probably refuse to accept your thoughts of love. In that case, those powerful thoughts of love will come back to you like a boomerang, and make you a fortress of love.

The reverse is equally true. If you hate anyone, you are sending the hateful thoughts to your enemy and friends alike, and as such you will become a fortress of hate.

Baptism and Upanayana

The Christian 'born again' concept is somewhat similar to the Hindu concept of Dwija (twice born) and the Hindu Upanayana ceremony.

Upanayanam represents **spiritual rebirth** and so it is called the **'Dwija'** or **'twice born'** ritual. Upanayanam is a Sanskrit word, which is made of two words **Upa** and **Nayanam** (vision through knowledge). Upanayana in is a ceremony performed to mark the point at which children begin their formal education in the Vedic tradition. The Upanayanam ceremony is completed with the wearing of the **Yajnopavitam** (Sacred Thread) on the body.

'Unless there is a complete change of consciousness from material to spiritual, nobody can attain self-realization.'

Does Hinduism Offer Me Freedom of Choice?

Why should I be a Hindu? Just because I was born in a family that practices Hinduism? Don't I have the freedom to choose for myself?

Unlike other religions, you have absolute right to follow Hinduism or reject Hinduism. You also have the right to condemn Hinduism in public and still proudly say 'I am a Hindu.'

Apart from that, Hinduism is a culture, a 'way of life' and is not an organized religion like Christianity or Islam. So you have the freedom to do whatsoever you want.

Remember, we are the only religion which allowed Atheists like Charvaka to openly condemn Vedas and Rishis.

Other Books by the Author

AM I A HINDU? THE HINDUISM PRIMER

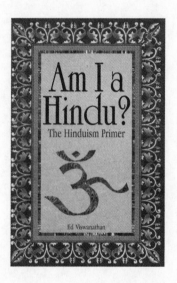

Here at last is a lively, compelling and truly informative book on Hinduism. Tracing this belief system from its ancient riverbank origins to its present day status as a major world religion, the book paints a comprehensive picture of Hinduism—rituals, festivals, epic tales, the caste system, scriptures, yoga and meditation, women's role, Hinduism and Christianity, the significance of modern science, and much more. Most of all, *Am I a Hindu?* takes the reader on a journey of discovery as it asks—and answers—life's most timeless and enduring questions.

AMAZING SECRETS OF THE BHAGAVAD GITA

Amazing Secrets of the Bhagavad Gita answers many commonly asked questions on one of Hinduism's most revered texts. It is not yet another translation or commentary on the Bhagavad Gita, but a topic-wise summary of the ideas and concepts found in the Gita. Topics as diverse as salvation, karma, chakras, yoga, abortion, creation and annihilation of the universe, how to deal with stress, how to pray, gambling, Avatars, and more are discussed and explained for the lay reader in a simple and effective manner. The lively conversational style between a grandfather and his eighteen-year-old grandson makes it an easy and engrossing read.